THE LEG DEBATE

THE
LEG DEBATE

A NOVEL

Jason Medici

MEDICI PUBLISHING WORKS

CALIFORNIA

Copyright © 2017 by Jason Medici

All rights reserved.
Published in the United States by Medici Publishing Works, California

ISBN 978-1-732-01420-6
eBook ISBN-10: 978-1-732-01421-3

Printed in the United States of America

Book design and cover by Jason Medici
www.jasonmedici.com

10 9 8 7 6 5 4 3 2 1

First Paperback Edition

PART ONE

ONE

Dresden Industries boasts the largest and most state of the art laboratories in the country, and why wouldn't they? It was no secret that wonders flourish inside those walls – the Calcunists saw them as miracles. Fashion of the times dictates that it's no longer enough to be. Progress, constant and ever evolving, is necessary.

The world is dull and boring. This was, of course, decided long ago by a popular vote no doubt created for some political purpose of the day. Though the purists adamantly maintained that life had already reached perfection long before man's intervention, they were tolerated by the rest of the world rather than exalted. And while purists adamantly disagreed, it was determined that life should be a foundation for the new. The possibilities were endless. And with a skilled imagination, a black and white world could be given color.

Why settle for an original apple when some fruits were now entire meals? Science brought the world into the era of change. Under the microscope, anything was possible. The deformed were corrected and made whole. Take a serum and obesity transformed into the waistline of choice. The wrinkled and old found beauty restored. Eden was today.

David Allens carefully buttoned up his jacket taking extra care not to skip a hole. Such a task should be rudimentary for a PhD geneticist and the youngest recipient of the cultivation grant at the tender age of twenty-nine, but it took effort with the mind engaged elsewhere. He put on his glasses and wiped a strand of brown hair off his face. It fell right back in the same place. That's alright, he told himself. Dresden didn't hire me for my looks. And besides, I'll cut it off when I get to work. He always reassured himself in the same way but had yet to see it through. He swung a satchel over his shoulder and headed out the door.

With little to spend on rent, the commute to his new job at Dresden Industries wasn't as short as David would've preferred. But all the same, he was glad to take the forty-five-minute metro ride as well as walking the twenty minutes in between stations for the opportunity that was certain to open countless doors. He grabbed coffee and croissant on the way.

The city of Ambris was a lively place to live. The young and ambitious alike gravitated around for the many opportunities it offered. Cultures were diverse. Whether one identified as a purist, calcunist, or even gypsy, they were certain to flourish in such a dynamic atmosphere.

Unlike Rhune, the city's northern metropolitan counterpart, Ambris welcomed all walks of life. It was as common to see a calcunist sitting in a café voicing the numerous benefits of advancing the world through evolutionary manipulation to a gypsy as it was to witness a head-covered purist silently lamenting the loss of creations beauty as he walked down the street. Though they took their devotion seriously and never left home without a hat, onlookers merely saw identifier as an easy way to avoid potentially awkward conversations.

Most purists frequented the temples at least twice a week. A moving experience for many, it was also a chance to be social. The temples, resembling museums more than anything else, contained preserved specimens of plants and animals as they once were. Before the establishment of human interference that was marked by the day scientists first cross-pollinated flowers, the world was considered pure. Animals were not enhanced, people looked as nature intended, and plants were perfect in their simplicity. The temple exalted these beliefs with an unspoken gratitude towards The Quiet One – a creator without a true name, only known by her collected works of the planet. Obviously a she as Her womb was where Her followers believe all life originated, The Quiet One could never have an equal.

Outside of the metro, many gypsies made temporary homes. While some were well off with large houses and a number of other luxuries, others flooded in from around the world hoping to build a life starting from nothing. Neither purists nor calcunists at heart, they appreciated life without the need look towards the future or a previous time. Walking past a young family gathered under a splayed overhanging tarp, David tried not to look all the while hoping his glasses hid the frequent glances in their direction.

He never did understand other religions. What makes people willing to praise and put their faith in the flawed designs of nature when the promise of something better was being shouted from the rooftops? Maybe it had to do with a lack of education. After all, gypsies new to Ambris weren't known for sending their children in for advanced studies. But despite all their faults, and he could think of many, at least that young family wasn't as bad as the Purists. Though he would never say such a thing out loud, David knew deep in his heart this to be a truth.

As a geneticist, David had a great admiration for the basic building blocks of the world. He even appreciated the construct of the world as a foundation. But to solely advocate life with that level of simplicity was beyond irrational, it was completely absurd. A rose bush that only produces flowers of a single color was certainly pretty, but it was unimaginative and even boring when compared with the newly-designed bushes displaying multiple colors on each individual petal. Progress through beauty is the true reason for praise, and no one would be convincing him otherwise.

The commute to work was as lively as any other workday. An enormous billboard advertised the latest youth regeneration procedure with a female model in the process of molting. As the skin fell away, so too did years of wrinkles, sun damage, and age. Emerging from the discard was a woman far younger and happier with eyes that knew more secrets than youth could ever collect.

Passing the park between stations, David watched a man taking his dog for its morning walk. He had always wanted one of these modern creatures and had waited for the opportune moment before producing one of his own. Constructed with precision in every aspect, the medium sized dog had nails that grew to the desired length before the growing mechanism was switched off. The animal's short, white hair never shed.

"Play?" The dog suddenly asked as it looked at the man with hopeful eyes.

"Not right now, Thomas," the man replied. "We'll go home first and have breakfast. We can play with your ball after."

"Okay," the dog said before its ears perked with the sight of a cat resting on a nearby balcony.

An internship in his fifth year of studies allowed David to work on increasing the size of the dog's brain. Even then, he had been amazed at the newfound ability to comprehend basic words and thought processes. Another department, specializing in vocal reconstruction, then gave the animal the ability to voice its thoughts. The result was an endearing companion that understood the world through the eyes of an eight-year-old. Back then, David had taken notes and was fairly certain he could increase the brain activity to that of a fifteen-year old. But such a thought led him to keep the research to himself since nowhere in the world was there a market where a perpetual adolescent was desired.

Arriving at Dresden Industries just before nine and announcing himself to the guard at the front desk, David received an identification badge and attached it to the front of his jacket. It wasn't noteworthy as everyone in the building was required to wear the same thing, but David's chest swelled under the subtle weight.

To him, it was more than just a badge. Years of striving and sleepless nights studying had brought him to this point. It had all been worth it, and he wore the badge with pride. As a member of the group, he was now capable of so much more. Instead of academic theory, he was expected to take strides and make advancements. The challenge was daunting, and he was eager to get started. David made his way to the elevators and pressed the button.

Honeysuckles filled the air. Faint but present, the illuminated numbers above the steel doors casually descend all the while David was unable to find the source of such a pleasant scent. His mother's garden immediately came to mind. When he was little, the boy spent countless hours in the back garden next to a wall covered in honeysuckles. Bees were rampant, buzzing in and out of the little white blossoms, but they never bothered him. He and his younger sister used to pull the pistil from the center and touch the drop of nectar to their tongue. The scent was unmistakable and yet an absolute mystery. With only two small trees growing in the entry way of this massive construct, neither produced a single flower.

The elevator doors opened, and he trailed a group inside the confined space. The smell continued to linger. Floors one, two, and three emptied out the majority until only he and a woman remained. It was then that the aroma became stronger, and he looked at the source with surprise.

She was younger than most of the employees and couldn't have been past her early thirties. A pair of glasses magnified her bright brown eyes. Her hair, parted down the center and pulled back into a bun, exposed delicate ears that seemed to remain oblivious to the faint music playing through some hidden speaker. Her red blouse was layered with a white cardigan and tucked delicately into her black pencil skirt.

Empty handed with fingers folded together and thumbs playing a game of their own, she looked around the confined space aimlessly all the while entertaining herself with a pocket of air expanding and contracting in one cheek. Then, unable to take it anymore, she turned her head in David's direction and gave him a polite smile as if to say, you're staring and I'd rather you didn't. Suddenly aware of his lingering eyes, David curved his lips attempting a smile of apology and looked away.

They reached the fifth floor, and the elevator doors slid open providing an escape route for what had become an awkward situation. David stepped out and tried not to notice that the woman was right beside him. Both continued to walk in silence completely aware of the other's presence. Unsure of who was following whom, they gave each other an occasional smile all the while walking side by side to the office of Lucas Germond's personal assistant. David was becoming flustered and could see the same emotion spreading across the woman's face. Was there some mix-up? They continued to put on an air of professionalism all the while secretly hoping the third-party's presence would not cause a poor reflection on their own persons. The assistant picked up a phone and announced their presence before quickly nodding. "Mr. Germond is expecting you," he said with a smile. "Go on and head inside."

"Come in, come in," Mr. Germond voiced excitedly as the pair entered. "Our newest additions and two of the brightest. Miss Alice Clarke," he said shaking the woman's hand. "The pleasure is all mine. So accomplished and still so young! If half of my scientists had a mind like yours, society would be ahead by at least a century by now. I love the perfume! Is it a chrysanthemum composition?"

"It isn't perfume," she remarked with a warm yet shy smile. "My mother loved honeysuckles and had the flower spliced into her DNA. I was able to inherit the gene and became a second-generation flower."

"Remarkable! Your mother's reputation precedes her! And I believe she personally wrote your recommendation for this position. You may be her daughter, but if she has confidence in you as a scientist and is willing to put her reputation on the line, that speaks volumes."

From the look on Alice's face, it was clear that she was flattered. At the same time, she knew herself to be an underling – forever to live in the shadow of her mother's success. Alice, no doubt, struggled to reach new heights in a futile attempt for the world to see her as her own person. Whether or not she was to succeed remained to be seen, but the determination in her eyes made it clear that she would stop at nothing and try with every ounce of strength she possessed.

"And David," Mr. Germond said taking the man's hand and giving it a shake. "Dresden Industries is ecstatic to have you! I could see your brilliance during our last interview, and I daresay my expectations for you are some of the highest I've ever had. I have no doubt a stroke of genius will come from your combined efforts."

"Combined?" David asked curiously as Alice's face reflected the same surprise.

He and Alice looked at each other with confusion. It was clear that both were under the impression that the laboratory would be theirs alone. The idea of sharing hadn't even crossed their minds. But here they were. Suddenly making sense of the situation, both knew the opportunity was too good to pass up regardless of whether or not they'd be sharing.

"Oh yes," Lucas replied with the same enthusiasm. "Wherever you two choose to begin, genetics and gene manipulation are tricky fields to accomplish any real progress. It's going to take more than just skill which you both possess – it'll require vision.

By yourselves, I'm sure each of you would do well and add new products to the market. But together, my hope is to produce something exceptional. I hope this arrangement won't scare either of you away, but I wholeheartedly believe this could be the beginning of something exceptional. Can I count on you both to pursue the extraordinary?"

The pair glanced at each other giving the other a moment's calculation nodding in unison.

"Splendid! I assume you're both anxious to get started. Get to know each other and brainstorm. The lab will be ready this afternoon, and your badges will give you access. If there is anything you need, please come to me directly. I practically live here, and my assistant, Mr. Orwens, but everyone just calls him Martin, is just as dedicated and readily available."

After voicing final words of gratitude for the opportunity, David and Alice took their leave walking side by side back to the elevator. The air felt tense. There would be countless conversations between them, but neither could figure out a way to break the ice. As the elevator took them down a couple flights and the smell of flowers came back to the forefront, David kept his eyes forward.

"My family used to grow honeysuckles in the garden behind our house," he told her all the while doing his best not to make eye contact. "Sorry for staring earlier, but smelling something so familiar after all these years really took me by surprise."

"It's okay," Alice told him picking up on his attempt at conversation. "It's not a very common scent anyway. My mother developed a whole series of flowers to be added to DNA, but she never put the honeysuckle gene on the market. I guess she wanted to be unique and the only one of its kind. I don't think she ever expected to share it – not even with me. But life is funny sometimes."

"I thought about getting some work done," David admitted casually. "But it's still a bit pricey for someone straight out of college. Maybe I'll look into it in a couple years after working at Dresden. In the meantime, I'll have to keep appreciating the fragrant aroma of laundry detergent."

Alice couldn't help but laugh. Her mouth curved into a smile while she looked at her feet shyly. "You want to know something?" She asked ready to confide a great secret. "Honeysuckles are tainted for me. The less I shower, the more I smell like flowers. After an hour at the gym, I could be mistaken for a garden of my own. Even though I smell nice, I don't feel clean. That's why I wash my clothes more than anyone else."

"I always thought the point of constantly smelling good was to cut back on laundry days," he said amusedly.

Alice shook her head. "Because my body is different, my mind developed with a different perspective. It's one of the unforeseen side effects of gene manipulation. We practice the physical but ignore its mental implications. Resequencing DNA may be the easy part. Making the mind accept the change without a negative opinion is where things get tricky. I haven't quite figured that part out yet."

David thought for a second. "So what you're saying is that, whatever we decide to create, we should probably avoid adding a flowery scent."

Alice giggled with the same downward glance to her shoes. "Absolutely."

TWO

Dresden's cafeteria, if one could call it that, only reflected a small portion of the dining area. It had a variety of dishes ready to order, and employees generally took their meals back to the offices and laboratories to continue working without interruption. The plates were made of a new strain of potato, banana peel, and hemp. Once discarded and introduced to high-frequency sound waves, the dishes broke down to create mulch used in every garden around the facility and packaged for global distribution. The trees and other foliage grown in such soil proved that the sustainable design worked marvelously.

The majority of the food area was occupied by a restaurant simply known as The Rendezvous. Always busy but never completely full, employees could always find an empty table to meet with coworkers, take a break from the long workday, or develop new ideas over a gourmet meal. So popular and with such delicious entrees, a section of the restaurant recently opened its doors to accommodate the public twice a month on every other Friday. For those days, the public section had a waitlist nearly three months in advance. But it made employees feel good walking in without a reservation and eating just as any other day.

David was excited to try his first meal at The Rendezvous, but it would have to wait for another time. He and Alice took their seats in The Gene Pool which was the neighboring coffee shop. Alice had been running late that morning and was still in need of her daily caffeine fix, and David was happy to oblige.

One bite of the cranblue scone convinced him to never again eat them anywhere else. The cranberry-blueberry hybrid was common enough to find anywhere in the city, but the difference in taste between any vendor and The Gene Pool's was obvious with packaged cranblue berries versus a batch freshly harvested from the water.

"I've had assistants, but never a partner," David confessed.

Alice took a sip of coffee and shrugged. She had expected to brainstorm entirely on her own. But instead, she was back in her usual position – as just another part of the team. Her mother had always been the leader, and everyone else provided the bodies to see the vision become reality. That was the past, she reminded herself. Here, she was a leader on equal footing with the man across from her. Whatever vision they had, they were both in charge.

"This is new for both of us," Alice told him. "I'm sure we both have different styles, but we'll make it work."

"Where did you even come from?" David asked in admiration of her cool head.

She wanted to punch him, but that was probably not the best way to begin things. I've always been here, Alice wanted to scream. Just because I've been living in a shadow doesn't mean I came from nowhere!

"I took the usual route," she said casually. "University followed by a couple years working on various projects. But this will be the first time I'm tasked with creating something entirely new. Any ideas on where to begin?"

David thought for a moment all the while scanning the room for any sign of inspiration. "Curing diseases would be a step in the right direction. Or we could enhance the efficiency of the stomach. Maximizing nutrient intake could put an end to world hunger."

Judging from the polite smile on her face, David instantly knew both his ideas were instant flops. That's okay. He came to the same conclusion as soon as they left his mouth.

"Those both have obvious benefits," Alice said trying to choose her words as carefully as she could. "But I don't think they'll grab as much attention as we're looking for." Unable to think of where to begin or come up with an idea of her own, she looked at her coffee without another word.

"I guess you're right. It's just a little daunting being tasked with changing the world."

"I know what you mean," she confessed.

"We could always ask your mother for ideas," David said jokingly. "It would be an interesting experience working with the famous Martha Clarke."

I could strangle you for even mentioning her! Alice thought while revealing nothing more than a controlled smile. From his tone, she could tell that the man was teasing. But it still struck a nerve. Her mother wasn't someone she wanted to add to this conversation. And even though the list of applicants to work with her celebrity mother grew every day, Alice preferred to think she wouldn't be forced to share a lab with one of the groupies. It was a joke, she reminded herself. He knows we don't need her help and is only joking. She took a deep breath through her nose and subtly exhaled her insecurities.

David looked at her name badge and then to his own. Taking it off and looking at the Dresden Industries logo, he couldn't help but laugh.

"Improving the world one day at a time," he said reading the company moto. The world has already been improved so much. Any thoughts on where we take it from here?"

"That's really the question!" She said excitedly. "What else do we want in the world? What do we want in our future that doesn't exist yet?"

"More rocket ships?" David said amusedly.

Alice rolled her eyes but couldn't help finding the humor. "We're geneticists. Let's leave space to the astrophysicists and concentrate on what's on this planet."

David continued to look around before suddenly standing and swinging his satchel over a shoulder. Alice looked at him curiously all the while wondering if he had been offended by her comment, but the smile on his face told her otherwise.

"The world is already littered with coffee shops," he remarked. "And they tend to be very similar. If we're going to look for something original, we have to be out there seeing what needs to change. Let's go for a walk outside. Something is bound to spark an idea."

As much as Alice wanted to make herself comfortable in the new lab and put a wall between her work and the outside world's interference, something inside agreed with this approach. There would be plenty of time to forget about the rest of the world later. Once looking through the microscope, she was always good at doing that. But for now, they needed ideas. She took a large gulp of coffee and left the empty cup on the table before following him outside.

The bustling area outside of the building contained some of the most well-kept streets in the entire city. Walking areas lined with trees and bushes splayed in every direction leading to various buildings, business parks, restaurants, and public transportation lines. It was beautiful in its own right, but one look made Alice certain that creative inspiration towards something completely unique could not be found in an environment so controlled. She led the way to the metro and took it a couple stops north.

When she and David emerged, they found themselves across the street from the river that flowed directly through the city's center. Gypsy children played on the banks while calcunist mothers let their young ones laugh and run around on the playground just beyond. Without any real destination in mind, he and Alice took a seat on a street bench. David pulled a notepad and pen from his satchel all the while looking around for anything inspirational to spin the wheels in his mind.

"Algae that eats away unwanted bacteria and pollution," he said while scribbling down a note.

"That already exists," Alice reminded him and watched as her partner put a line through it. "How about water that doubles as a food source?"

"I'll make a note, but I don't think it'll draw the kind of attention we're looking for."

Alice thought for a moment. "What kind of attention are we looking for exactly? It has to be amazing, but what does that really mean?"

"It has to better our lives or take the world in a new direction," David said after a moment's thought. He looked at the children splashing in the water and laughed. "Maybe we should focus on creating amphibians. I'm sure the kids would love that."

"That's actually not a bad idea," Alice commented giving it some thought. David could see a light switching on in her mind. It had started with a joke, but from there was taking on a life of its own. "Think about the possibilities. Living above and under water has obvious benefits. And why stop there. If we're restructuring ourselves to get the most benefit possible, let's look to nature for other possibilities."

"What do you have in mind?"

The woman looked at a bus parked on the corner taking on a load of new passengers. Each with a different destination, they shared the need to get somewhere faster than humanly possible.

"I took the metro this morning, and the first car was completely full. I had to wait an extra seven minutes for the next train to show up. And everyone does it just because we can't get where we need to fast enough – even if it's only a couple blocks away. People take the metro and buses because they're direct and fast. What if we weren't restricted by navigating through a grid? What if we could take direct routes anywhere we need to go and get there faster than our legs allow?"

"You want to create superhuman legs that can travel at the same speed as cars?" David asked putting down his notepad and focusing on Alice curiously. She shook her head.

"Wings."

"Wings?" He asked as if hearing her correctly was obviously out of the question. "You want to give humans wings?"

"Think about it. Before we grow gills and have the same traffic congestion underwater, wouldn't it make sense to perfect life on the surface first? There would still be trains and planes for traversing long distances; but for everyday commutes, we could make life easier for the masses."

"Unless you want to see mothers getting winded flying around with three children in their arms, they'll still need cars and public transportation."

"But it would be reduced radically. Only the people with children would be its regular riders. Everyone else would get to their destinations as quickly as they choose."

It had obvious potential. Even though the thought of working with a partner had been an initial shock, David could see what Mr. Germond was talking about. They were already making a great team. If their work in the lab was as progressive as their brainstorming session, a breakthrough was certain to take place. The look of excitement in Alice's eyes only increased his own thrill for the days to come. This was the first time a conversation had so naturally fallen into place that he could remember. Though reserved but trying her best to step into her own light, Alice appreciated the same.

THREE

The day had gone incredibly well. David and his new partner spent hours walking the streets discussing the pros and cons of altering the human form all the while thoroughly enjoying their first day at a new job. It was more than simply transferring animal qualities to people – such things were common practices from regrowing human limbs using lizard cells to improving eyesight developed from the eye cells of predatory birds. Even the standard sex change took no longer than introducing the enhanced frog genes into the body and letting them run their course. What was on the table, for all intents and purposes, was the next stage in human evolution.

Was it possible that mankind had reached a plateau in its development? Of course there could be significant improvements to the basic design, but primary constraints remained in effect. Evolution and progress walked hand in hand requiring change, but would humanity become something better by such development or would the animal genes used in the process make the most significant stride forward? Such questions kept them talking long after the workday ended and the evening commute home was underway.

It was well into the evening when David opened his apartment door just in time to see Milo scampering towards him and ready to jump. A moment later, the little brown dog was in David's arms, tail wagging with the excitement of company.

"I missed you!" The little Yorkie voiced with an obvious smile. David smiled back and put a finger to his lips reminding Milo of the need for silence. He put the dog down and closed the door quietly.

"You're in a good mood," the man said setting Milo on the ground and his satchel in the corner. "Did something exciting happen today?"

The dog spun around. "My football team made it to the playoffs! A couple more wins and the Ambris Griffins will be in the semifinals!"

David couldn't help but laugh at his friend's excitement. It was certainly unusual for a dog to take such an interest in sports. But then again, Milo was the furthest thing from ordinary. David had created him in private several years ago. Hoping for so much more than the norm, he had succeeded in giving Milo a mental capacity far beyond anything in production. Milo was three, or twenty-one in dog years. And his mind was still developing. Where it would stop was a question even David couldn't answer.

"Did you spend the whole afternoon down at the pub watching the match?"

"You worry too much," Milo told him. "I know the routine. If anyone says something, I pretend to be as slow as Daniel downstairs. 'Daddy is coming to take me home,'" he said in slow and obvious mockery.

"Sometimes I wonder if some cat genes accidentally made it in your mix. You're the only dog I know that patronizes other dogs, and most of them don't sneak about finding creative ways to watch sports."

"Most dogs don't practice a civilized sport in their spare time," he retorted.

"Are you ready for dinner?" David asked as he made his way into the kitchen. "There's some leftover fish if you want it."

Milo followed close behind. "I read an article this morning about how fish used to be the leading cause of mercury poisoning. Are you trying to poison me?"

David looked at him in disbelief and rolled his eyes. "They sorted out that mess nearly twenty years ago. I think it's safe." He pulled the leftovers from the refrigerator and thought back to the idea of growing gills. "If you had the chance to live underwater, would you take it?"

Milo tilted his head to the side and looked at David without saying a word. They had been together long enough for the man to know when his sanity was being called into question. And without a single word, Milo was doing just that.

"It was just an idea we came up with earlier," he explained. "It would certainly change things."

"It would make eating tonight's dinner an act of cannibalism," the dog told him before jumping on a chair and having a seat. "But what do you mean by 'we?' I thought you always work alone."

David took their plates to the couch and rehashed the day's events while they ate. Maybe it was always easier for him to talk to animals rather than people. With Milo, he knew he could confide the secrets of the world and they would be kept safe. Even with the gifts of understanding and speech, the dog was still his best friend. And though he preferred to focus the conversation on his work, Milo picked up subtle hints better than anyone else and would pester enough to always have an answer.

"Tell me more about Alice," the dog said while scratching an ear casually with its back paw.

"There's not a lot to tell," David said leaning back. "From what I've heard, she's a brilliant geneticist. We spent all day discussing work, and I think we're really onto something."

"What is she like?" Milo pressed. "Tell me something about her."

David thought for a moment. With so many ideas floating through his head, it was only after Milo's helpful snap back to reality that he remembered their first encounter. He talked about her natural scent of honeysuckles and her first smile. There was something about her laugh that made him gravitate in that direction. And when he noticed Milo resting his head on folded paws with eyes looking straight past his fumbling words, the man took off his glasses and closed his eyes. Milo would never let something like this drop. David waited for the inevitable.

"You've got a girlfriend! You've got a girlfriend!" The dog sang.

David kept his eyes closed and smiled at the ceiling. "She's my lab partner. Let's leave it at that."

"I can hear your heart beating faster when you think of her. You should tell her how you feel."

"I just met her today," David voiced with a laugh. "And besides, I'm still trying to recover from making a fool of myself this morning in the elevator. Maybe I should've made you into a cat. That way I could tell you anything and you still wouldn't pay attention to a single word."

Milo licked David's hand and climbed up on his lap. "You're joking, but I will bite you so you know it's in bad taste."

FOUR

For a Tuesday morning, the streets were oddly crowded when David left the metro station near Dresden Industries. Instead of the usual bustle of commuters, there were people of all ages filling the streets and sidewalks. All with their heads covered, it was a purist rally. Posters were raised above their heads. 'Perversion is not perfection', 'The Quiet One is without equals', 'What comes out of laboratories isn't really alive' read a few of the signs. Feeling more than a little uncomfortable, David cautiously tucked his name badge inside his jacket.

"David?" A voice called from somewhere behind.

He spun around seeing no one familiar – only hats and signs. Suddenly from nowhere, an arm locked with his by the elbow and began dragging him forward. It took a second for David to find the source. The man, covered in a brown hat, moved as discreetly as possible. When the stranger glanced to the side, that was all David needed to instantly recognize the familiar face. It was Mr. Germond's personal assistant.

"You're a purist?" David asked as they left the crowd a couple paces away from the building and found safety behind the thick walls. "I didn't think your religion approved of this kind of work."

The man smiled to himself as he removed his hat. "I was born and raised a purist, but I'd say my religious beliefs are a matter of perspective. Not all of us are as strongly opposed to progress as that lot," he said gesturing toward the crowd.

"What's that all about anyway?" David asked knowing full well the assembly wasn't the sort of thing to happen on a daily basis.

"Didn't you watch the news last night?" Martin asked in disbelief. "The government is considering whether or not to approve human cloning. No one seems to mind an exact copy of a heart or kidney for transplants. But as soon as someone mentions copying more than just a body part, this is what happens. I was only out there to check in with my godson, Gregory. He likes to be part of these kinds of things; but still, I'm hoping he grows out of it."

He looked at his watch and started walking to the elevator. "I really must be going. Mr. Germond's phone will be ringing off the hook this morning, and the unhappy task of organizing his schedule to respond to this demonstration falls on me."

Left alone, David headed to the fourth floor and swiped his badge granting access to the lab for the first time. Seeing his and Alice's names on the door made him smile. It was theirs. Everything inside was solely for their success. Whatever happened behind this door would be a mystery until the partners decided to share it with the world. Once inside, he immediately took off his jacket and replaced it with a new lab coat hanging on the wall.

All was perfect except for one thing. He left his satchel on the table before heading to The Gene Pool for his morning fix of caffeine.

Grabbing his coffee and looking at the many people still gathered outside, David's phone began to vibrate. It was Alice. She had just arrived to an empty lab and was wondering if he was running late. Sending her a quick response, he was on his way with all the excitement of a five-year-old ready to play with his new toys.

"Did you see the crowd outside?" Alice asked as soon as David came through the door. He nodded all the while wondering if it was possible not to notice something so obvious. "Honestly, you'd think those people would have better things to do than stand around protesting what's in their best interest. Or maybe cloning another person isn't actually in their best interest. I don't know."

"What do you mean?" David asked taking a seat and sipping his coffee. Questioning any advance of science certainly wasn't the sort of thing he had ever expected a fellow scientist to do. "You don't think it's a good idea?"

Alice looked at the table and thought for a moment. Her fingers picked absentmindedly at the corner of a barcode sticker left on an empty binder.

"I'm all for progress, but I guess I don't really see the benefit in cloning an entire person. If it's for the sake of body parts, the brain should be left out it. But to create an exact copy of someone seems more like a way to stoke the ego than anything else." She peeled off the sticker and began folding it smaller and smaller. "I think the challenge of it is thrilling, but to decrease the value of the original by making a copy seems pointless."

"That sounds like something a purist might say," David pointed out. "Isn't that what they're arguing outside?"

"Don't worry. I was raised a calcunist and have no desire to convert. But I think the ones outside are more concerned with any comparison between humankind and The Quiet One. They don't like the idea that a creation isn't different and can't be criticized. If we produce an exact copy, they wouldn't be able to argue that we finally reached the point of creating perfection. There would be no difference between us and their Creator."

"That doesn't sound so bad," David said after thinking it over. "Maybe we are gods in our own right. If we can do the same things, maybe they'll finally put their archaic beliefs to rest. It would decrease the red tape every time we take a step towards something new."

"If we're only making strides to compare ourselves to The Quiet One, then everything we do is for our own ego rather than to better ourselves as a society. We would be more interested in possessing the ability than simply being. I think cloning a person for the sake of it falls in that category."

Even though he wanted to argue, David couldn't think of any retort. As a calcunist, he always believed that progress for its own sake was admirable and something to strive for. People had crossed his path expressing their concern for ingenuity over the years, but he rarely noticed them. They didn't fully comprehend what was at stake. It's wasn't like they were real scientists. But with Alice, he couldn't help but wonder how such thinking had worn off on a fellow geneticist.

"If a family loses their child, shouldn't they be able to replace him?"

"I don't think a way of replacing to the full extent actually exists," she replied thinking it over. "We're still talking about the creation of another person. That child would still be dead. And no matter how much the clone looks like and is an exact replica, he would still be someone new. And the family would still remember what happened to their original child."

"That sounds like a choice better left to the families," David said feeling slightly uncomfortable having a conversation he had never before taken seriously. "Our only role in the lab is giving them the option."

"Perhaps," she admitted. "Maybe you're right. I'm usually much more objective, but something about giving a clone to some desperate parents breaks my heart."

There was something in her eyes that David couldn't quite place. Sorrow had risen to the surface from depths unknown. Whatever was the cause affected her considerably, and the man knew that if they were going to make any progress today, this melancholy had to be put back in its place.

"Are you okay?"

Alice looked up from her moment of absent-mindedness and saw David's concerned expression. Was it really that obvious, she wondered? Her partner was nice, even charming at times. She could talk with him for hours about things that wouldn't make an ounce of sense to anyone else, and they connected. Despite meeting only yesterday, it felt like she had known him longer. It was a feeling she didn't have a lot of experience expressing; but behind her guarded veil, she felt it. Truthfully answering his question still felt impossible, but she appreciated his concern anyway.

"I'm fine," she told him and forced a smile.

Honesty to that extent would have to wait for another day, she told herself calmly. How could she share her real concerns about the cloning issue? Maybe cloning did have real benefits for families in need of replacement children. But what she feared most and did not dare to voice was what it would mean if anyone had dared make one of her.

The thought sent a cold shiver up her spine. She had always strived to be the perfect daughter. But her mother being who she was, would an exact clone of her little girl be enough or would the woman see it as an opportunity to improve the many faults unspoken? Would she be smarter? Taller? Would her clone still smell like honeysuckles or would that mistaken inheritance be rectified? Alice wanted so much to agree with the purists and believe that she was one of the many acts of perfection or live as a gypsy and find beauty in the present. But despite her desires, she was too clever.

The next few days were devoted to sketches. Neither were artists, but they tried their bests to get the ideas across. Once it had been decided that their laboratory project would be a type of evolution for mankind, they were left to figure out exactly what such a mission would entail. Both agreed on wings, but whether or not feathers were necessary was a source of ongoing debate. And why stop there? Wasn't it in everyone's best interest to be able to see further, think clearer, and hear with new sharpness? Getting rid of man's original role of the dice, nothing was left to chance.

After Alice's strange reaction to the cloning conversation, David had been extra careful to avoid letting ego have any role in their work. Undertaking such an endeavor admittedly gave him a sense of pride, but he refused to let it become anything more. Making it clear that they were creating something new seemed to improve the work days. And as long as their work stayed clear of duplicating an aspect of flawed design, Alice maintained enthusiasm.

As talk about the cloning issue died down in the media, the crowds eventually died as well. Government officials assured the public that a date to discuss the issue had not even been set. And in the meantime, each opinion would ultimately be taken into consideration. The purists were satisfied for the moment but continued to circulate petitions further solidifying their position. All other religious practitioners tried their best to avoid that headache-inducing discussion with purists positioned on the streets ready to recite from a script the merits of signing their petition.

With so many strong opinions about the right direction of the world, no one was surprised when a group known as The Horsemen suddenly emerged. 'One step closer to purity' could be found painted on the sides of buildings, and it was no secret that the culprits had done something to progress their agenda inside.

The first newsworthy attack happened at a plant laboratory. In the many greenhouses where cross-pollinated flowers were being developed and enhanced further, a series of explosions filled the air with a lethal dose of nitrogen. Instead of finding sustainment in such a chemical, the plants were nourished to death within minutes. A note was left on the door. 'Gluttony is your undoing.'

The news covered a series of disasters two weeks later when the serum used in sex-alteration procedures was found to be contaminated with a human agent. Though the procedures were still a success, the patients' new physical appearance had all become that of the same person. And without careful study of how the serum had been corrupted, doctors would not risk being implicated in a failed reversal. Without any options, the unlucky recipients walked around with the same face until the government's emergency reversal procedure came into practice later that month.

Though the sex-reversals were successful, the contaminating agent was never clearly identified. Without knowing the full extent of the sabotage, a government-mandated disposal of all sex-alteration serum put an end to the service until a new batch could be created and tested for purity. It was only after the announcement of the final containers of serum being destroyed that The Horsemen left a message outside of Dresden Laboratories. 'The Quiet One creates perfection the first time.'

FIVE

Mr. Germond was unusually apprehensive as he sat in his office across from David and Alice. Though he tried his best to maintain a professional appearance, worry was bottled up beneath the surface. Hiring this pair was supposed to be a milestone in his life's work. Nurturing the genius in two extraordinary thinkers could record his name in history as a fascinating figure himself. With so much on the line, he didn't want to scare them away just because of a few incidents and religious fanatics.

"I've had some time to look over your proposal," he said opening up the folder containing David and Alice's sketches, genetic speculations, and research direction. "In all my years sitting behind this desk, never have I come across a project of this magnitude. It redefines humanity altogether, and I'll confess that I'm astounded you're willing to commit to such an undertaking. Do either of you have any concerns for where this might lead?"

David and Alice had sat quietly waiting for Mr. Germond to take the lead. Had their proposal caused the man's agitation? He had asked for something bold and newsworthy – that's exactly what they delivered. But was such an idea stepping over some imaginary boundary? David swallowed hard and watched as Alice glanced in his direction hoping he'd do the speaking.

"It's certainly unconventional," David began. "But that's why we're here, isn't it? We were brought on to make real progress for the world. I can't think of a better way to do that than help mankind with an evolutionary transition towards something better – remarkable even."

"Remarkable is a good word for it," the man admitted. "Brilliant is another." The pair let out sighs of relief when the curve of a smile spread across their employer's face. "This is exactly the kind of ambition I was hoping to see from the pair of you. It's bold, imaginative, and for all intents and purposes is the very reason this company was created. You have no idea what an exciting moment this is for me right now."

He flipped through the sketches before taking a moment to examine a rendering of a full body. "Wings and a tail seem to be the biggest changes," he continued. "How did you come up with that combination?"

"Wings were the biggest improvement," Alice commented while a little nervous that the scent of honeysuckles was practically radiating from her body with each drop of sweat. "The feathers will mirror the person's natural hair color; and with any luck, flight will be the answer to our congestion problem on the roads. The tail became necessary for better control in the air."

"That makes sense," the man agreed with a nod of his head. "But that will require a significant amount of control over the tail at all times. I remember reading about an unusual combination you were planning to use for this purpose."

"An elephant trunk structure," David added instantly. "Since we want complete control over this new part of the body, we'll be creating the tail from our own design. We'll be using a gene sequence found in elephant trunks and reconstructed to produce a tail. It'll have a thin layer of hair to protect against accidental damage and be capable of far better dexterity and coordination than all of our other limbs combined."

"And it'll be smaller than an actual trunk?" Mr. Germond grinned.

"Yes, sir."

Why the need for another appendage? The director asked curiously.

"It's the same principle as adding a tail to a kite," Alice remarked.

"Aren't legs sufficient?"

"They are, the woman confirmed. "But for correcting minor weight distributions while in flight, it's much easier to move a tail to one side than to have a pair of legs flailing." Mr. Germond laughed under his breath before nodding and returning to the page. "We did make some crucial changes to the legs," Alice pointed out. "They may look the same, but the new muscle design will have real benefits with a more active lifestyle."

"...one that involves flying," David added simply.

"The purists are going to love that," Mr. Germond said amusedly with the faintest lines of concern. "At least those Horsemen haven't gotten wind of this yet. We'll of course be making a public statement; but with something this important, I think it's best to add several new layers of security to your facility and this entire building. And with any luck, that group will be apprehended long before we make our announcement."

Though The Horsemen's behavior had worried David with each new antic, his safety didn't feel like a real concern. After all, the group was known for messing with lab products and creating disorder. Accumulating a human capital through violence certainly wasn't part of their description. When their project went public, he and Alice would be safe. Their lab would be secure and keep their research safe.

The pair was glad when the meeting ended. After two months' worth of preliminary designs and practicing gene splicing sequences, the work could continue. Desperately in need of a drink, they headed to the local bar a couple blocks away to celebrate.

For mid-afternoon, the place was already busy. Happy hour wouldn't come around for another three hours, but many workers in the area were anxious to get started.

Though the bar smelled of sweet cocktails and beers on tap, David noticed the honeysuckle aroma that hovered around their table. He had picked up on the smell even before the meeting in Mr. Germond's office. He knew Alice was sensitive about it and didn't want to say anything to jeopardize their proposal; but now, after a couple months of working together, taking their meals together, and finding kindred spirits through like minds, something as trivial as the floral smell was no longer off limits when they were alone.

"It went well," Alice said in between sips of a peach and pomegranate cosmopolitan. "I think it went well. What do you think?"

"It went well," David agreed.

"I knew you'd say that. Cheers to the future!"

Their glasses clinked as they kept eye contact. David felt the cool minty taste of his mojito drain down his warm throat before it created a moment's chill in his stomach. It was over as quickly as it had begun, and the man found that his body accepted its second sip with a newfound eager delight.

One drink led to two and then a third. The hours flew by before it really was happy hour which was all the more reason to keep the celebration going. A woman sat alone at a table across from them. Nursing a drink and occasionally flipping a loose strand of blonde hair away from her face, she gave David an occasional glance before returning her attention to a stack of papers.

David could feel the woman's stare. On more than one occasion he had looked in the blonde's direction to see her looking up suddenly and giving a subtle smile as if he had been the one looking at her all along, but this wasn't the case. Even Alice had looked in the woman's direction at least twice before returning her attention that much more fixedly on David.

Alice didn't like that this woman was interrupting they're celebration. It wasn't right. For all the blonde knew, she was interrupting one of their dates. Of course they were only lab partners, but she didn't know that. It was infuriating. Alice tried to lean across the table making sure David's eyes remained on her.

But what was she really doing, Alice asked herself while laughing at one of David's clever jokes? They worked together. Why did it matter if he looked at some random stranger neither of them would ever see again? Of course it mattered, she told herself haughtily. She didn't know how exactly, but it still mattered just as much. Feeling the effects of the alcohol and needing a break from the desire to give the blonde a confrontational stare, Alice excused herself to the bathroom.

Once the door was shut, she looked in the mirror and fixed her makeup. Her lips looked a little dry, and so she put on a bit more lipstick. Alice could smell honeysuckles reeking from her pores. She sat on the toilet taking a moment to calm her nerves.

Things would go back to normal tomorrow, she told herself. It was all the stress of the proposal and skipping breakfast that morning. With everything else going on, having low blood-sugar wasn't helping. That was it. She was just hungry. Finally getting a handle on things, she would head home, make some dinner, and enjoy the weekend without this sudden pang of jealousy. She straightened her skirt and felt better being back in control and with a plan.

As soon as the door opened, the smile faded. There was a slight fingerprint on the edge of her glasses. Alice had forgotten to wipe it off while in the bathroom. But even with the minute distraction, she could still see David. Though he was still seated just where she had left him, it was the blonde woman with a hip leaning against their table that immediately made her see red. Had a conversation begun as soon as she was out of the room? From the look of things, not a second was wasted. If that's how she wanted to play, Alice thought while putting on a calm air, two could play at that game. She confidently traversed across the room and wrapped her arms around David playfully.

"I think I've had too much to drink," she said and could see the blonde watching them contemptuously through the corner of her eye. "Would you mind helping me to a cab?"

Surprised at the feel of her arms around his neck, David also felt a sudden thrill. The honeysuckle aroma enveloped him, and he could practically taste its sweetness with Alice's lips only inches away from his face. He could feel the heat radiating off her body. He always imagined her hands feeling that soft.

"Of course," he said making an effort to focus on her eyes instead of her lips. "Alice, this is Evelyn," he said lifting his nose in the direction of the blonde. "She handles legal work for progressive scientific patents. I imagine we'll be working with her pretty soon."

"It's nice to meet you," Evelyn said without missing a beat and extending her hand to Alice.

Work certainly was a good excuse for sex, Alice thought while keeping the smile on her face and shaking the woman's hand. Both women looked pleasantly at each other all the while imagining the other's demise. "It's nice to meet you too," Alice countered. "I'm so sorry you couldn't have been with us earlier to celebrate."

"Maybe next time," David added pleasantly.

Both women kept their smiles glorious while silently clenching their jaws.

Grabbing their jackets, David put on arm around Alice's waist and helped her outside. The feeling was not lost on either of them. Alice wanted his arm there just as much as David couldn't bring himself to remove it. When a cab arrived and the thought of David returning inside to continue his conversation with the woman became too much to bear, Alice pulled him close for a hug and thanked him for the afternoon. And before even she knew what was happening, her lips had found his and were savoring the moment.

Though surprised, David couldn't pull himself away. The taste of her lips was a nectar of its own. Her lips were fruity, and the texture of her tongue made David want to feel it again and again. He was addicted. After so much time spent together and desiring what was never voiced, he never wanted to be without her again. Suddenly their kiss ended, and Alice looked at him with desire.

"I'm not really that drunk," she admitted with a grin. "But I could still use some help getting back to my apartment."

"We've spent the whole day together already," he said still unable to remove his arms from around her waist. "You're not sick of me yet?"

She kissed him again and breathed in his scent.

"I'll let you know in the morning."

SIX

Subtleties never escaped David, and waking up next to Alice presented him with a myriad of subtle details to take in on what was obviously a glorious Saturday morning. Her bedroom was sparsely furnished but filled with objects. There was a hairbrush on the table next to the mirror, clothes hung in the open closet and were shoved indiscriminately in a row, the nightstand was overflowing with books of all sorts, and a bottle of perfume rested on a shelf just beside the door. Alone, they meant nothing. But together, they painted a picture of the girl beside him.

In a bit of a hurry the night before, their clothes had made it as far as the floor. David vaguely remembered Alice attempting to put her glasses on the nightstand, but it was a hopeless effort when his hands and lips had been exploring her body. Trying a second time would've yielded the same results, and the glasses wound up landing on a shoebox just below.

He didn't want to wake her. In fact, he was more than content just staring. Something about the way Alice slept accentuated her beauty, her kindness, her perfection. In that moment, she was perfect. Far from a purist as David was, something inside made him certain that The Quiet One had gotten the formula right when She made her. There was nothing he would change. It seemed silly to strive for a world with wings and ambitions when this very room was all it took to give his life meaning. He could smell the honeysuckles coming off her body and breathed in deeply. Perfection.

"You're staring," she mumbled in the early morning light. Alice's eyes remained closed and yet a smile had spread warmly across her face.

"I can't help it," David told her before kissing her neck tenderly. "Flowers are meant to be admired. And since you smell like one, I have no choice but to look and appreciate."

Her eyes stayed shut, and she frowned playfully. "Are you saying I need a shower?"

"Don't go anywhere," He told her wrapping an arm around her naked torso and pulling her close. "Stay right here. I'm enjoying this way too much."

"Me too," she said and finally opened her eyes.

A strand of hair fell over her cheek, and David playfully used his nose to push it off her face. The world was quiet and peaceful. The woman let out a giggle. The world was as simple as that.

Including another person into David's life after so many years alone should've been more of a challenge, but it came naturally. Maybe it was their working relationship that had eased him into the situation, or perhaps it had more to do with so many laughs shared and existing feelings unspoken that made this step something logical. Whatever the reason, he and Alice found their time outside of the lab equally enjoyable. And last night's development meant more than ever.

It wasn't until mid-afternoon when they finally left the apartment. David needed to get home to check on Milo; and Alice, being the closet animal lover that she was, decided to go with him. Though happy enough to have the company, the man was unsure what to expect. He trusted Alice. Shouldn't that be reason enough to let her in on the secret? But then again, Milo was one of a kind. But his hand was warm in hers, and one look in her direction gave him the answer he needed. David unlocked the door and immediately heard the familiar scampering across the wooden floors.

"I'm so hungry," Milo said while excessively wagging his tail and taking in the sight of the stranger. "Please feed me before I die."

"Awww, you poor thing!" Alice said kneeling down and letting the dog smell her hand. "David, when was the last time you fed him?"

"Years," Milo said as he put his front paws on her for a better look.

"He can feed himself when he's hungry," David informed her while shutting the door. "And the look of that stomach seems like he didn't skimp on supplies. You can drop the act, Milo."

"So hungry," the dog continued trying to get at face level with the woman. "Please feed me before it's too late. I can smell steak from a restaurant nearby. If you bring me some, I'd be ever so grateful."

The woman's eyes grew wide as she looked from David back to Milo. "Did he just…"

"…try to pull a fast one on you? Yeah, he did."

"He just formed a complex thought," she continued in amazement. "That's extraordinary!"

"Milo isn't your average dog," David admitted. "I made a few enhancements outside of the normal procedure."

"You're making me sound like a lab experiment," Milo said bluntly.

"You know you're not." David said scratching his friend behind the ears. "You just have a better thought process than any other dog out there. Granted, your obsession with football was a surprise. But to each his own."

"You like sports?" Alice asked with surprise.

"Just football. That and tennis are the only two sports they show at the pub downstairs. But listening to the players scream every time they hit the ball wears on my ears."

"You're a dog that likes football," Alice commented incredulously trying to make herself believe it.

"It's amazing having a real conversation with a dog doesn't make you gasp but knowing that I like football does. You have been cooped up in the lab for too long, Alice."

"You know who I am?"

Milo looked at David with an expression that could only mean mischief. "Of course I know who you are! Unless some other woman smells like honeysuckles, I've heard a lot about you."

"Oh really?" She said flashing an amused glance at David. "What's David been telling you?"

"I long for the days when animals were seen and not heard," the man commented.

"All good things," Milo responded knowing he had Alice's full attention. "But I don't think David has mentioned the most interesting things – like why you smell like him for example." Milo smiled happily watching the woman's complexion adjust by two shades of red.

"C'mon, Milo," David told him. "Be nice."

"I'm always nice," he countered. His expression was sincere and sorrowful, as if the very notion of him being anything but a truly caring soul had hit him at the core. He stared into Alice's eyes with a look that made her melt. "I just want to know. Are you going to be my mommy?"

"Oh my quiet one," David said taking off his glasses and rubbing the bridge of his nose. "You actually went there."

Of course the answer was yes! How could anyone say differently staring into eyes so cute? But then again, he was engineered, Alice thought to herself. Everyone played to strengths, and Milo was no different. Did that really matter though? If he was really asking if she wanted to be part of a family, it made no difference if he used everything in his arsenal to get the answer he desired. The thought hit her like a sudden charge of electricity. He wanted her in the family. That must mean David had mentioned it as well. She could feel another shade of red coming over her.

"This may be the first time we've met, but I've had a long time to think it over," Milo continued. "If David is as crazy about you as he pretends not to be, then I want you around also." He gave her a big smile displaying his pearly white teeth. "Take as long as you need to think it over. We'll be here. And in the meantime, we really should be on our way or we'll miss kick off."

"We're here for lunch. Not to watch football," David commented.

"The pub does serve food, you know."

"I think it sounds fun," Alice said suddenly, and both looked at her with surprise.

"You're a football fan?" David asked suspiciously.

"Not exactly," she admitted. "But it's Saturday, and what else do we have to do? And besides, how else am I going to butter Milo up enough to give me all the juicy details on you?"

"I'll tell you everything," Milo insisted.

The man shook his head incredulously. "As a precaution, his vocabulary is drastically limited outside. It's better if he doesn't draw any unnecessary attention."

"I'll whisper," Milo urged.

Looking from one face to the other, David had no choice but to cede. His dog looked so hopeful, and Alice was obviously delighted by the prospect. There was no harm in letting the two get to know each other. In fact, he had been hoping for as much for some time now. The circumstances had played differently in his head, but reality being the fickle thing that it is decided differently.

The pub was packed on game day, and David had to hold Milo for nearly forty-five minutes before a table opened up for the three of them to claim. Though there was more than one pet in the place, Milo was the only animal trembling with excitement every time the Ambris Griffins were about to score.

Milo did live up to his word. Though he spoke in something barely above a whisper, the dog divulged more than one secret to Alice's eager ears. Every woman loves to know what her lover does when she's not around, and Alice was no different. From their walks through the city to late night get-togethers with his friends from university, Milo left nothing out. The woman was interested in all of it. And much to David's embarrassment, the dog heard more than he had ever let on.

It was strange for Alice to feel like part of the family. She would have to figure out their work relationship later. For now, they were just another couple having lunch with their dog. And that was all she wanted. Ambition was her route to importance, but a moment's happiness meant nothing more than feeling David's hand on her knee and keeping up with Milo's enthusiasm. It was a very good day.

SEVEN

Alice stayed the night; and when David left to meet an old friend for coffee, the woman opted to stay behind and have some personal time with Milo. She was utterly fascinated by his ability to think and comprehend. Every word that came from his mouth represented something to be explored. But instead of viewing him as the newest science project, David could see her looking at Milo as if he were a child in need of being understood and nurtured. Though unorthodox, the interaction was good for both of them. Before heading out the door, David set the rule not to tell her anything humiliating. But he knew it was to be broken within minutes anyway.

Calvin Shettler was one of David's closest friends. They had taken their first year of university together before classes separated them for the remainder of their studies. But they had always made a point to meet up and grab drinks, chase girls, or chat pleasantly about the direction of their studies. Though both geneticists and engaging conversationalists about the latest scientific advancements, things had become a bit dull for Calvin when his latest form of income came from customizing gene sequences for women to have the permanent appearance of wearing makeup.

"We can't all have Dresden Industries practically begging us to work for them," Calvin had said when asked about his work in cosmetics. "Let's face it. Unless geneticists, chemists, and all other scientists for that matter make names for themselves by the ripe old age of twenty-five, they're stuck living a life of customer service. 'Yes ma'am, I can give your lips a permanent natural swell and redness in any shade you like.' 'Of course, sir, we can suck your ginormous stomach and fat ass right out of your genetic makeup so they'll never come back.'

'I'm sorry, little girl, but it's our policy to have your parent or guardian sign a consent form before we resequence your DNA so you grow larger breasts.'" He gave his coffee a stir. "Customer service at its finest. And all us average lab techs look on as people like you get to practice the real science."

"Don't sell yourself short," David told him. "A hundred years ago, they had surgeries for everything. If your arm accidentally got chopped off, they fitted you with a prosthetic and told you to go on with your life like nothing changed. Now we regrow the limb, and that's the customer service you provide. It may not be pushing boundaries, but it's life-changing for the ones that don't need to go through life minus one appendage."

"Is it really life-changing for them? It's become the norm, and I practically work on an assembly line. If a person loses a limb, they no longer think of it as a big deal. What's the need for panic when you can get in line and grow another?

"There's a young couple that are regulars for me," he continued dryly. "They always get lost in the wilderness trekking up some ice-covered summit and usually lose a few toes to frostbite in the process.

"Last month was a bit more severe. The man had so much damage on his right foot that we decided it was easier cutting the whole thing off and having him grow a new one. And his wife had to grow a new ear, cheek, and nose to replace her black ones. Is it really life-changing that we operate a convenience store to replacing damaged goods, or are people more reckless because a foot is no longer one of a kind?

"Don't get me wrong. I enjoy helping people. That's why I got into this business. But I have to wonder if this is all there is to life – returning a fragile body to optimum condition just to see it fall apart again just because no one bothers to treat it with more care."

"Maybe they need to be reminded to care," David said after a moment's thought. "They're pushing the boundaries of their own physical limitations trying to reach something unattainable. But that won't stop them from trying. And if it takes sacrificing an arm or leg to get one step closer to living, who's to say they don't have the right idea all along?"

"Are you saying I haven't fully lived my life because I still walk around with the same set of ears my mother gave me?" Calvin asked with a grin.

"In your case, I can see why you kept them. I think we can agree those can't be replicated no matter how good the science. But for everyone else, maybe they could do with a bit more living instead of so much focus on how to stay alive and in peak condition."

"You sound like a gypsy," Calvin laughed. "Living in the moment is well and good until there's something about the present that needs to change. So they fix whatever needs fixing and then go on praising the moment like nothing ever happened."

David looked around making sure there wasn't anyone in earshot that might overhear their conversation. "They really do baffle me. Some of them live on the streets with nothing while others could pass as calcunists any day of the week."

"They have a way of blurring the boundaries," Calvin admitted. "Gypsies grow replacement parts and take cosmetic serums as often if not more than any other religious group. You'd think personal development was a rite of passage and act of worship the way they frequent the dispensaries."

"Would it really be so terrible for the lot of them to put their faith in ambition and progress like any other calcunist? They're obviously more than happy to use our innovations whenever it serves their needs."

"That would certainly make the most sense. But then again, you'd be asking people to choose a religion based on objectivity and logic. If you're going to use that argument, perhaps you should have a conversation with the purists while you're at it."

David couldn't help but laugh. "I don't think The Quiet One would approve. She's never been the most practical or logical of sorts."

Calvin was suddenly quiet as he frowned at the empty cup of coffee-superfood that would keep him nourished for the entire day. His brow furrowed with a thought just beneath the surface. It traveled to his eyes and hung there like a barrier blocking all other projections. Lost in its scope, he stared at the picture of the table without seeing any of it at all.

"What's on your mind?" David asked sensing the change of mood.

"My sister, Nancy, has been seeing a guy for a few weeks now. He's nice enough – a purist with some pretty interesting beliefs. Normally I wouldn't give two thoughts about a creation story, but his stuck with me probably because it's so progressive."

"When I think of The Quiet One," David commented. "Progress isn't the first word that comes to mind."

"My thoughts exactly. But like I said, this isn't your average purist story."

David sat upright giving Calvin his full attention. His hands folded together on the table, and he sat quietly with a smile on his face waiting for the story to begin.

"Instead of a single Quiet One, there were three. Each of them had a specialty. One knew the water, another knew the earth, and the third knew the air. They took it on themselves to fill these areas with all sorts of creations."

"Three creators?" David asked trying to wrap his head around the concept.

"Doesn't it make more sense than a single woman giving birth to all life in her gigantic womb? And if there's anything you and I can both agree on after years of playing with DNA, it's that genetic codes do not easily carry over from one species to another."

"But they do have similarities in parts," David reminded him.

"That's true. But I think of genes as a kind of living language. They contain a certain number of letters that can produce an astronomical number of words and phrases that are each individual for a particular concept, trait, or physical attribute. And when we want to enhance genes to give us, for example, the ability to shed our skin like a snake, we string together the existing letters in a new order to produce an entirely new word for our purposes. The letters might all be the same between species, but the words are entirely distinct."

"In light of this new information, does this mean you'll be converting to purism?" David asked with a smile.

"I don't think there's a real chance of that happening," David scoffed. "Whether it's one Quiet One or three, I still prefer looking towards the future instead of the past. She or they might've been exceptional creators for their time, but I like where we've gone since then. And as any headstrong calcunist will tell you, the world is better off leaving those relics in the past."

David was about to agree when a loud crack and intense rush of air flew in his direction. Glass from the windows was rushing towards him, and the other occupants were flying out of their chairs. It took less than a moment's glance at his friend's upside-down body before a pain in his eye made David wince. Something hard hit the top of his head, and that was the last thing he remembered before the blackness.

EIGHT

David's shoulder ached. He wanted to move it but felt too spent to put forth the effort. Every ounce of energy was drained. His back was stiff from lying in the same position for who knows how long. A quick stretch was in order, but all he could manage was moving his tongue and tasting a buildup of morning breath that had been accumulating for some time.

His finger felt pinched. Though initially only a slight discomfort, the more he thought about it the tighter the grip became. Soon it was unbearable. He opened his eyes only to see blackness. It was too warm to be nighttime, David reasoned. Unsure of where he was or what was happening, he took a breath and lifted an arm. Aching from the exertion, he pulled off the small device clasped around his finger. An alert sounded instantly.

"David?" A familiar voice asked as soft hands reached for his. "Are you awake?"

It was a comfort to hear a voice so soothing, and the scent of honeysuckles filling his nostrils was calming. A faint smile touched his cheeks and made them throb.

"Alice," he said quietly and immediately felt the soreness in his throat.

"I'm here," she told him anxiously. He could hear the worry in her voice mixed with relief that he was finally talking to her. "It's good to see you awake. How are you feeling?"

He didn't really know how to answer that question. Parts of his body felt like he had fallen ten flights off a building while other areas were still a complete mystery.

"I've been better."

"David," Milo said in a voice that the man instantly felt compelled to comfort. "Are you going to be alright?"

"I'll be fine, Milo," he said into the blackness. His eyes itched, and he let out a groan to make them stop.

"You're finally up," came a man's relieved voice from somewhere in the room.

"David," Alice said. "This is Doctor Pulmer. The hospital assigned him to you right after the accident."

"Accident?" David asked. He remembered finishing his coffee with Calvin and then the rush of wind throwing everything into disarray.

"There was an explosion," Alice told him. "That radical group everyone's been talking about, The Horsemen, they put a bomb in the veterinary brain enhancement clinic. Thankfully, it's closed on Sundays and the building was completely empty. But the blast from the explosion reached the café across the street. You were brought here right away. That was three days ago."

"You're lucky to be alive," the doctor commented while occupied with other matters in the room.

"If you had enough of me, you could've just left that morning," David said with a grin. "A bomb is a bit excessive. Don't you think?"

The man could hear Alice's laughter mixed with a pang of overwhelming emotion. She placed her hands on his chest gently. David could feel her wet cheek next to his and the tears in her breathing. She gave him a tender kiss trying to hold back her fear.

"Don't even joke about that," she told him. David felt a tear land on his chin. "And I'm not done with you yet so you have no choice but to get better."

"Why can't I see you?" He asked as the itching in his eyes worsened. "Everything's black."

"Your eyes are wrapped during the healing process," the doctor said casually. "You'll experience a bit of blurred vision in one eye while it heals, but the other one had to be replaced entirely. Too many little pieces of glass made it beyond fixing, and I don't know a surgeon who would even make the attempt to fuse together that many pieces. Besides, you'll like the new one much better anyway."

"I checked the tissue sample and gene sequences myself to make sure they're a perfect match," Alice told him. "You'll make a full recovery."

"Let's have a look at your working eye and see how it's coming along," the doctor said adjusting the bed to a sitting position and carefully loosening a bandage. "I can honestly say I've never had a patient check and then recheck every cultivated tissue and serum used on such standard procedures, but I suppose that comes with the territory when you're regular practitioners. Seeing her devotion to your recovery would've been enough to turn me into a calcunist if I wasn't one already. There you are," he said removing the last piece of gauze from one eye. "Give it a try, and we'll take it from there."

David's eye fluttered as he opened it slowly. It was dry, and blinking a couple times gave it lubrication after what felt like an eternity of being stuck to the underside of his eyelid. His vision was clearly still on the mend. Shapes and colors were distinct while clarity was haphazard at best. But through the blur, he recognized Alice's hair. She was right beside him with a look he couldn't quite bring into focus. The fuzzy brown spot at the foot of his bed could only be Milo. Even through the fog, it was good to know his best friend was with him. The doctor's black hair and white lab coat were close to the corner of his eye. Though the figure was fuzzy, the proximity was still too close for comfort.

"It looks like everything is healing just fine," the doctor told them before taking a step back and making some notes on a clipboard.

"When can he leave?" Alice asked with urgency.

"It probably won't happen until tomorrow," he said without taking his eyes off of the clipboard. "Since growing a new eye is far more complicated than replacing a finger, I'd like to keep him here one more night. By tomorrow, he should begin to get eyesight. I'll discharge him as soon as that happens. In the meantime, just rest and let your body heal itself." Without another word, the doctor returned the clipboard to the foot of the bed and closed the door on his way out.

"Finally, he's gone," Milo said crawling up the bed until he could lay his head on David's ribs. "I don't trust him. Something about his smug expression makes me want to bite him. And he smells like a cat person which isn't earning him any points."

"The only thing that matters is that he fixes you," Alice commented. Her blurred face was eyeing him up and down – taking in the extent of his injuries and briefly glancing in the direction of his vitals on a monitor.

"Well I'm not leaving David alone with him," the dog insisted.

David gave him a pat on the head and tried his best to conceal the pain in his shoulder that came with it. But somehow, Milo sensed it and moved his head a little closer.

"Where's Calvin?" David asked suddenly remembering he had not been alone in the cafe. A glimpse of his friend flying through the air was all he remembered before everything went dark.

"He's alive," Alice told him at once. "But he hasn't woken up yet. He took a pretty hard hit to the head during the blast, and his brain started swelling. The doctors put him in a coma until the swelling goes down and they get him stable. But he's alive," she reassured him. "Calvin's just in rough shape at the moment."

David sat speechless. It was wrong. Everything about this whole episode was wrong. What had he and Calvin done to deserve any of this? What had anyone else at the café done for that matter? He had always been careful about how critical he sounded towards other religions while in public, but that decency had only landed him here in a hospital. He was now in the process of growing a new eye because only one side was playing by the rules.

Alice's warm hand on his brought a tear to his one working eye. David was angry and could feel a growing hatred for The Horsemen and anyone who encouraged that behavior in the slightest. But part of him could feel the woman's hand and wanted to concentrate solely on that. He was split between yelling and shouting at the injustice of the world and crying from the realization that he had come so close to death. But her hand was on his, and it rested there giving him peace.

"Thank you," he said looking at the blurry Alice beside him. "Thank you for being here."

The woman picked up Milo and took his seat on the bed beside David. The dog didn't seem to mind. She placed him on her lap all the while giving in to some hidden nurturing instinct her grandmother must've passed along before she could even remember. A fuzzy hand wiped the tear from his eye as she nodded.

"I know," she said trying to be brave and holding back what flood laid beneath the surface. "It was just as hard on me and Milo when we heard the news." Her voice seemed to catch, but she forced herself to continue. "The television was on when a news report flashed to the café you and Calvin were at. We got there as soon as we could, David. It was a mess. And when we finally caught up with you, you were already in surgery."

She couldn't hold it back any longer. The days of constant worry and horrific scenes of the aftermath of the café felt too heavy, and Alice was collapsing under the weight. She could barely breathe.

During that eternity between hearing the news and reaching the hospital, she and Milo had been uncertain whether they would find a thoroughly used punching bag or a corpse. For all they knew, David had already been put in a drawer until funeral arrangements could be made. The thought was devastating. He was brilliant and had so much more life to live. Their work and the world couldn't continue without him. But even more than that, he was her David.

Yes, David was hers, she thought suddenly and was certain that this was true. They worked together which had kept their relationship professional for the longest time. But in the same way calcunists view positive changes in the world, their relationship had evolved into something better. And it was to be praised. Though sudden as it was, Alice had dated enough wrong guys to recognize the right one. David fit the bill. And wherever this was leading them, that's where she wanted to be with her hand in his through it all.

David could barely make out the shine as tears streamed down her face, but the sound of Alice's strained breathing was all too clear in his ears. Whatever had happened to his shoulder, it would be sore for days. But that didn't stop him from reaching out and pulling her closer. Alice could barely feel the force, but she didn't object and laid her head on his chest while the tears continued to flow.

He wasn't going anywhere, David reassured her. Now that he was awake, the worst had already passed. Kissing the top of her head, he suddenly became aware that his own cheek was wet from tears of his own. But Milo was one step ahead. And before he knew it, the dog had found a way off of Alice's lap and was licking his face dry.

NINE

The road to recovery wasn't an easy one, but David had help along the way. From the moment he left the hospital, Alice was by his side. She picked up his medications and even brought him a change of clothes. It was a treatment that was unfamiliar to David, and he was all the more grateful for that reason.

During his days spent unconscious, David had given little thought as to how Milo had managed. With a dog smart enough to hold conversations, having him take care of himself was never an issue. There was an enormous reserve of dog food at his disposal with just the push of a button. Milo came and went as he pleased using the small flap on the bottom of the front door, and he had proven to be resourceful on more than one occasion especially on days sporting matches were being aired downstairs.

But as soon as David set foot back in their apartment, it was clear that the bachelor lifestyle Milo was accustomed to living had been discontinued for a time. The kitchen was cleaner than he had left it, the dog toys were all put in their basket instead of strewn across the floor, and a stack of folded blankets and a pillow were neatly placed on the side of the couch. Beside it was an overnight bag that clearly belonged to a woman. The pieces fell into place with surprise, Milo had had company.

Gratitude swept over him as David watched the blurry shape of Alice set her purse and his medication down on the counter. Without thinking, he crossed the room and took her in his arms. "Thank you," he said softly in her ear. He could feel her smile against his cheek.

"The couch?" He asked looking at her a little amused. "You know there's a perfectly good bed in the other room. And I can't see myself objecting to you being in it."

"It wasn't your feelings about it that I was concerned with," she told him while her eyes subtly glanced towards Milo who had already found a miniature football to kick across the floor with his paw. "With everything that happened, I didn't want to give the impression that I was somehow replacing you. And besides, it was only a couple days."

"Well now that I'm home, the bed is readily available to you."

"That's a relief," she said smiling. "The couch wasn't nearly big enough for me and Milo. He really is a bed hog, you know."

"He slept with you?"

"Neither of us wanted to be alone while we worried."

"No need to worry anymore," he assured her. "It's over."

He took a seat on the couch and took a deep breath. Putting on a good face was the easy part. The near impossible task was convincing himself that things could go back to normal. He had held it inside since the moment he woke up, and the feeling had been growing. But the worst part was that he wasn't sure if what he was feeling was anger or fear.

"I've been in contact with Mr. Germond," Alice said casually while fishing in her purse and pulling out a tablet. "He's more than understanding given the situation. He told you to take as long as you need to recover. And in the meantime, I can recheck our existing gene sequences in the lab."

"They're fine already," David told her knowing full well they'd both been meticulous in their calculations from the beginning.

"I know that. But unless we choose the second option, I'll still have to find something to do."

"There's a second option?"

"I know you're still on the mend," she began with a smile. "But sometimes the best way to take your mind off of everything else is to concentrate on some work. I know Mr. Germond will agree, but I wanted to run it by you first. How do you feel about working from home? We can create the physical genes once you're back on your feet and in the lab; but until then, all we really need is a computer to keep working on the structure and pairings."

"You want to set up one of our lab computers in here?" David asked curiously.

"Not exactly," she confessed. "Since I wasn't sure if you wanted to work from home, I had them set up the computer at my place. But you have to admit, it'll be a lot more comfortable working from a bed or couch instead of a lab chair. What do you think?" She asked taking a seat beside him on the couch.

Thinking about how he was feeling, David knew she was probably right about burying himself in their work. The alternative would be dwelling on those mixed emotions which was something he certainly didn't want to become an everyday occurrence.

"It's a great idea," he told her.

Alice looked at her hands and smiled to herself. She had known it would work. But until David gave his official approval, she still had that lingering anxiety and would continue to wonder if it was in fact such a good idea. All that was now long gone. And the only thing left to do was get him better and continue where they had left off.

"I stored a lot of our research on my tablet," she said swiping through the screens until the right information showed up. "We'll obviously need to run the gene sequencing simulations on the computer at my place, but this will work for all the little stuff."

The pair began to put their minds to the task at hand and very quickly fell back into the swing of things. David found it to be therapeutic working again. Though his eyes still couldn't see very clearly, he managed without them. He visualized the concepts in his mind; and thanks to Alice's interpretations, they were constructed digitally that very moment.

"The Horsemen aren't going to like this one bit," David said half-jokingly.

"They don't have to," Alice responded curtly. "Why people think it's okay to bomb a building is beyond me. We're not going back to the Stone Age. What's the point of even trying?"

"Maybe it's what The Quiet One demands," David shrugged.

"That's ridiculous."

"Is it? Purists spend hours in their temples reminiscing about a time none of them were even alive to witness. And for some insane reason, they think that was the real Golden Age when life and creation were perfect. I'm not saying it's right. But if they're adamant to change the world back to the time fresh from the womb, then they must believe that's what their religion demands of them."

"You've given this a fair amount of thought," Alice commended though still unwilling to accept that religious extremists had the brain capacity to produce such an analytical perspective.

David had a choice, and he felt it in that split second of silence. He could either let her know the truth or let the topic die as nothing more than a passing thought. It felt good to talk. But at the same time, he wasn't sure if he was ready to get it off his chest.

"I have been thinking about it," David at last confessed while looking at Milo kicking the ball.

For some reason, he felt too embarrassed to make eye contact. "I need a reason. I have to know why."

"Why what?" The woman prodded.

"I have to know why I almost blew up."

Alice suddenly understood, and she looked at him with new eyes. There was more going on beneath the surface, and she was seeing a glimpse of it for the first time. The happy face that was indifferent to the accident, she had known, was merely a facade. It would be strangely bizarre to think such an experience would not have an impact. And this finally was a glimpse of its affect. It made more sense than she cared to admit.

As a scientist, David looked for causes and effects. He needed a reason for everything. It wasn't enough to simply feel a certain way. He had to know why he was feeling it. Alice put down her tablet and put her hand on his leg.

"If The Quiet One does exist," she told him sincerely. "I doubt She would want any of her creations causing destruction."

"I believe that of you and me," David said calmly. "If you and I created the world, I know we would cherish it."

"Aren't we supposedly made in The Quiet One's image? If we feel this way, then so must She."

"The attackers are also in Her image," David reminded her. "We can't both be interpreting her feelings correctly. And they might be right. If The Quiet One does exist, who's to say She didn't create and now has a complete disregard for her creations?"

"If that's the case, it wouldn't be for all her creations - just the ones that aren't entirely of Her making."

"But hasn't everything changed to some extent at this point? There really isn't anything left that is an entirely pure design. Even the official date for the first cross-pollination probably wasn't the first time it happened. If The Horsemen are trying to interpret Her feelings and act accordingly, sooner or later they're bound to come to this same conclusion. The world will need to be purged completely."

David couldn't help but wince at this realization. Before The Horsemen, he had had theological disagreements with purists. But they were never a reason to question society's overall safety around its practitioners. What he was feeling now was the fear and anger once again mixing together into a nasty cocktail.

"Let's say you're right," Alice commented thinking the matter through. "The only way The Quiet One can have the world return to the point of first creation would be to systematically destroy the world piece by piece. But she is also a god that supposedly loves all her creation as her children. Why would She want any of it destroyed since it would cause her pain as a parent?"

"It's a flaw in Her design," David said with a smile.

Alice couldn't help but laugh. "Then she's not perfect. I think that goes against every ounce of purist teachings from the beginning."

"Who's to say they got it right when they created her? If nature is her template, then I think we should all be seriously worried about her sanity.

All animals in the wild live half starving lives and eventually die cruel and violent deaths. We're trying to domesticate the world just so that such things no longer happen. Parasites slowly kill their hosts, and diseases naturally ravage populations. If you and I were responsible for creating the world, I'm sure we would've perfected the design so that cancers and diseases weren't part of people's lives."

"That's why we have replacement parts," Alice said. "Every diseased organ can now be replaced."

"That's my point," David said feeling impassioned. "Everything we do to progress society has been to fix the mistakes from the beginning. All of our research and development has been to clean up the mess The Quiet One left behind. I think we need to take the design one step further," he said pointing to the tablet and suddenly understanding in which direction his thoughts had been swimming.

"What do you have in mind?"

"The human genes with their flaws are still too distinct."

"You want to make humanity less human? I don't think that's an option. If we're not using the base pairing, what is there to work with?"

David sat back and thought for a moment. There had to be a way, he thought to himself. Between the two of us, we should be able to...

It suddenly hit him, and a flash of excitement came into his eyes. They had been trying to create using what they believed to be The Quiet One's system of design. But if there was more than one god, then why shouldn't the best of all three make the perfect combination? That's what they were doing with the wings anyway. He finally understood how to proceed.

"Before the explosion," he said trying to put the flash of his friend's body moving helplessly through the air out of his mind. "Calvin was telling me about a different creation story where there were three Quiet Ones instead of just one."

"Three," Alice said incredulously.

Will nodded. "One made the creations in the air, another what's on land, and the third did the waters."

"Well, if you think The Horsemen aren't going to like what we're up to, I'd love to see how its members react when they hear about three gods instead of one."

"It's a bit out there," David admitted. "But I think we should be approaching our design as something unique where all the pieces can't be found in a single place. Instead of focusing on fixing the mistakes of one creation, why don't we use bits and pieces of various designs to produce something flawless. All we need are small bits of DNA from other species to make the new humanity disease-free. We're already doing this very thing to grow limbs, restore memory, and look young again. Why shouldn't we use this same approach to fix the root of the problems?"

"We'd have to do this in phases," Alice told him while thinking it over. "We can start with inserting enough DNA to get rid of let's say the top ten ailments and launch it as phase one. Who knows how many phases we'll end up with."

Alice picked up the tablet and immediately began drafting an email to Mr. Germond giving a brief explanation of their new direction. Her fingers flew across the screen tapping at the digital keys while reading aloud so David knew what was being written. He added input here and there; and when both were satisfied, the woman sent it off.

They had expected the message to take some time traveling through Mr. Germond's assistant before reaching him directly. After all, a man running an entire division of progressive industry could hardly be expected to read messages immediately. But strangely enough, it happened. Both were surprised when five minutes later the tablet chimed with the announcement of a new message. Alice picked it up and read aloud.

"All aspects are approved. Lab security is already in full effect. Proceed with caution."

TEN

It was an unexpected thrill when Calvin awoke nearly three weeks later. His doctors were uncertain whether or not he would ever regain consciousness when his eyelids suddenly parted. Though more than a little groggy, he was awake and coherent. David left Milo at Alice's apartment before rushing to the hospital the moment he received the news.

During David's recovery, a family dynamic had formed between himself and Alice that continued well after. They were still coworkers, but their first of many nights together had changed so many aspects of their lives. While David was still unable to see clearly, Alice had brought over meals for the three of them. And while she was out one afternoon, David had a spare key made. He gave it to her without asking if it was something she wanted. So many things were done without a single word. And they both thrived.

By the time the phone call came declaring the good news of Calvin's return to consciousness, Milo was more than comfortable spending yet another afternoon at Alice's apartment while the pair worked. After the explosion, David couldn't help but be a bit more protective; and since that meant Milo would have some company during his absence, he was grateful for the arrangement. Of course this wasn't without its offsets. Milo insisted on watching the matches in the other room. But aside from the occasional howl of joy or cry of hysteria, the two were able to work reasonably undisturbed.

It was nearly four in the afternoon by the time David reached the hospital. From the moment he saw his friend awake, he couldn't help letting a few tears escape from his eyes. Calvin was alright. After so much time wondering if his friend would ever wake up and if that would lead to a full recovery or a vegetative state, all had turned out well. David gave him a hug as if Calvin really had returned from the dead.

Though the man's recovery seemed far quicker than David's since he almost immediately he was able to get up and walk around the room with nothing more than a few cramped joints, they both knew it had taken significantly longer. After all, Calvin had been asleep during most of his recovery. And by the time he woke up, all the cuts and bruises had already long since healed. Physically, he had made a full recovery. But mentally, the terror of the cafe stuck with him.

His sister, Marcy, took him back to her place. It was another week before he returned to his own flat and went back to work. But once in the clinic, post-trauma swept over him like a wave. He tried to ignore it at first, but the longer he stayed in that potential target the less he was able to breathe. In the end, quitting was the only thing to do.

Much to Calvin's surprise, David was already one step ahead. Knowing his friend's personality and how such an experience would likely have long-term effects, David had taken it upon himself to get Calvin a job at Dresden Industries as a low-level blood analyst. It was some of the most tedious and repetitive work imaginable, but the labs were secure. It was an instant success. Calvin went back to work with a smile all the while knowing the doors remained sealed to all passersby and potential saboteurs alike.

But the fear of another inevitable attack was not restricted to Calvin or even to David for that matter. After the restaurant, gossip began to make its way around the streets that The Horsemen were gathering in numbers and ambition. Despite the collateral damage, some purists saw the attack on the veterinary brain enhancement clinic as a success and step in the right direction. They truly believed the group was being used as a tool yielded by The Quiet One Herself. If She had a plan for this world that would make all things pure again, destruction was seen as necessary. The Horsemen were growing in size, and the police couldn't definitively match a single face with the movement for fear of backlash from the entire religious community.

As a result, purists kept more to themselves. Calcunists tried to avoid associating with anyone wearing a hat or veil for fear that they might be seen as sympathizing with what was taking place, and they weren't alone in that concern. Even the gypsies who had remained loving of the world and neutral to progression and The Quiet One seemed to limit their interactions with purists.

The community uproar was severe when police announced that they would be monitoring purist temples to get a handle on religious radicalization. There were protests, and even calcunists voiced their concerns over what would happen if their faith in progress was suddenly under suspicion and innovation was brought under question. No one had answers, but everyone had an opinion.

The media frenzy focusing on religious rights and personal freedoms became white noise almost overnight when a press conference was held to announce Dresden Industries' most ambitious project. While Mr. Germond sat on stage with a panel of who's who in the organization, David and Alice sat just to his right. Holding hands under the table, both were nervous being thrust into the spotlight. The scent of honeysuckles gave away Alice's anxiety, and David poured her a glass of water whispering quiet reassurances.

Once the design for what was to be the new human was projected behind them for all to see, the questions immediately began to fly. With camera lights flashing from every direction, David and Alice kept their hands tightly together.

"It's just my opinion," a reporter began as he caught the panel's attention. "But that doesn't look very human. Can you give us an explanation why you think it's necessary for the world to look like that?"

"Believe me," Mr. Germond said speaking into a small microphone. "You're not alone in noticing the differences or questioning them. But this stage of advancement was chosen for a reason. It's creators, Doctors Allen and Clarke, I'm certain will be able to answer this question to your satisfaction."

Alice began taking a sip of water all the while giving David's hand a squeeze. She was looking down at the table, and David knew he would have to take the lead. Nervous as he was, the man did his best to give Mr. Germond a nod of acknowledgement before addressing the reporter.

"Picture the world around you," he began in a shaky voice. "Think about all the advances we've made to cater to our bodies as they currently are. We grow new joints and limbs to replace ones that have been damaged by wear and age. Our cities are filled with traffic congestion because our bodies are unable to get us where we need to go in a timely manner. There are serums to cope with, and in some cases, annihilate various diseases. All of these things stem from the same root cause. And to this day, we're trying to fix the flaws in mankind's initial design."

People began to mumble as soon as the words left David's mouth. Everyone on the panel had been expecting it, and the company publicist gave him an encouraging smile while subtly clenching her jaw. David took a deep breath and continued.

"What we have here is the next phase of human development. Instead of wasting all of our efforts adjusting to the limitations we currently have, we're eliminating the challenges altogether. Wings mean that the majority of private and public transportation will no longer be needed since we'll all be able to get ourselves where we need to go. Better joints and muscle structure mean that our bodies won't deteriorate nearly as quickly. And when it comes to sickness and diseases, we'll be eliminating those altogether."

"Imagine a world where cancer, arthritis, and even chicken pox don't exist," Alice said finding the strength to speak. "If it had been up to any of us in this room, I know we all can easily agree that creating a world without those ailments is preferable to wondering if one day you or your loved ones will fall victim. But we didn't have any say in how things were done in the beginning. And because of that, we're all forced to live with the consequences. But not anymore. This time, we have the power to make a world without cancer and to take the handicap out of the human design."

"If you take away the things we as humans have been forced to live with," a female reporter said with a hand in the air. "You'll be taking away part of the things that make us human. You'll be, in a sense, turning us into something else. Is that wise?"

"A person born one hundred years from now will be no more or less human than you are today, madam," Mr. Germond told her pleasantly. "But what we can reduce is the amount of suffering that people in the future will be forced to endure. The world will still present challenges. We, as a species, will still question life and wonder if there's more we should be feeling. But instead of spending so much time focusing on cruelties created in the past, we'll be able to focus on the future and answer questions yet to be asked."

"What will The Horsemen say about this?"

Someone had finally given voice to the elephant in the room. The question came from nowhere, and the room was silent in anticipation of the response. A pin could be heard dropping. Someone coughed. All eyes were on the panel. Glancing from side to side, Mr. Germond brought the microphone a little closer and spoke.

"From what I know of The Horsemen, they are opposed to all things considered to be advancements past the point of creation. There is no denying that what we are striving to achieve certainly falls within that category. Those of us working on this project all come from different religious backgrounds. We are calcunists, gypsies, and purists. We do not put one faith above the others and certainly have no wish to offend based on our personal interpretations of our faiths. But if The Horsemen come to the conclusion that all of our faiths and how we choose to practice them should be purged from the world, then such hate is beyond even the forgiveness of their Quiet One."

ELEVEN

"Do you remember Doctor Beteph's paper on limbs?" David asked one evening as the two sat lounging in Alice's living room with what had become nearly an empty bottle of wine. "I still have a copy back home somewhere."

"Of course," Alice replied at once. As a graduate student, it was primary reading for anyone researching genetics. An unpleasant memory crossed her mind when her mother had pulled the copy out of her hands and declared it to be grossly outdated. "It's clever as a paperweight but certainly won't prove useful to any real scientist," the woman had told her. Alice shook off the feeling and tried to remember what it said.

"…If we are to modify life from its original template," David quoted from memory, "we must first examine the intricate formation of all things. The reasons for locating skeletal structures internally versus externally, the quantity of primary organs, and the number of limbs are all examples of maximized efficiency…"

"…whether we define our humanity by our number of limbs is a source of ongoing debate," she said finishing the quote and giving a laugh.

"What do you think?" David asked thinking back to the leg debate every student in the last seventy years at one time or other examined and discussed over coffee, alcohol, or both. "Is it even ideal keeping the same number of limbs since we know the human design has its own shortcomings?"

"I remember my answer back at university, and I'll tell you the same thing now. It's what we know. Changing the count changes what it means to be human."

"But aren't we already doing that by adding wings and a tail?"

"More is better," she countered. "If we have four legs instead of two, we'll be capable of twice as much. With eight legs, we'll be capable of double that. We can't help redefining the species because physiological alterations will make us capable of that much more."

"Then we should at least give mankind an even number so we can be as creepy as spiders."

The woman gave a shudder at the thought. "Then we'd be spiders! No, thank you! Adding a tail and wings is enough. I still want to recognize myself when I look in the mirror. But we could always go the opposite route."

"Keep the wings and lose a foot?" David asked while refilling Alice's empty wine glass. "I'd feel too much like an amputee."

"That's the point, isn't it? We need two arms and two legs to keep us sane. We can add more, but anything less makes us feel reduced to something less than natural selection. But we could get rid of the skeletal structure altogether. We'd lose the fear of broken bones and grow eight tentacles like an octopus. And by enhancing muscle designs, we'll increase dexterity and strength."

"You don't want to look like a spider but have no misgivings reshaping the human design into an octopus? I can imagine a little girl scared of the monster under her bed dying of fright when her own mother walks in looking like something from her wildest fears. But of course, we can. Should we give them the option and let those with the strongest hearts be the only survivors of the initial shock?"

"Have it your way," Alice teased. "But remember Beteph's argument about working within the parameters of each species. '...If there is an unspoken law that we do not diminish or exceed our own capabilities, then it would be the single largest handicap to the community of innovation,'" she recited nonchalantly. "He makes a good point. I can see how easy it is getting carried away when this kind of floodgate is opened."

"That just seems like a clever way of appeasing the purists and avoid a burning at the stake. He wrote that paper nearly a century ago, and geneticists had to tread a lot more carefully back then. Change of any kind was always seen as a personal offence against The Quiet One. Thankfully, things found a way of calming themselves once the purists realized our scientific abominations could keep them young and pretty."

"Then we'll keep with that aspect and add six fins, horns, and a womb capable of carrying nine children at a time just to spite them!" She laughed.

"Of course, we could go entirely in the other direction and get rid of limbs altogether. There's nothing more peaceful than jellyfish. They're efficient, simple, and one of the most peaceful creatures on the planet. Who's to say moving towards the simple isn't a step towards progress."

"If The Quiet One had lived, She'd be turning in her grave right now. I really don't think that's what her followers have in mind when they talk about returning to the simplicity of creation."

"Our objective is to better society," he reminded her. "What better way of doing that than by splicing peace into the population? Perhaps the number of limbs is what compromised us from the beginning."

"Simplicity cannot equal perfection no more than complexity is synonymous with complication. We have awareness and choice. Whatever decisions we make have little to do with feet, tentacles, or a tail."

"But are we dehumanizing mankind by reducing the species down to a flaw? We're tasked with fixing the problem. Shouldn't we do just that?"

"We can cut away, splice, attach and manipulate the body until there's nothing left but immortality. But I wouldn't lay a finger on the mind. Whatever's in there is there to stay. We're no better at cutting out religion than we are at human desires. Whatever enhancements we do make, the finished product is out of our hands."

"Perhaps you're right," David agreed and drained what remained in his glass.

"Off to bed?" She asked through a yawn.

"You read my mind."

TWELVE

The lab door was equipped with the latest security. And to be extra cautious, the entire third floor now required special access granted only to those with identification badges. It felt a bit extreme; but given the ongoing threats, everyone felt safer knowing such security measures were in effect.

The moment the human development project announcement was made, The Horsemen had gotten wind. But instead of issuing a public response, the group remained out of the spotlight. Overly curious as to what this lack of action might mean, the media brought in religious experts, law enforcement officials, and human rights as well as purist activists to debate the question of whether or not The Horsemen philosophy and actions had some merit.

Horsemen sympathizers were known to frequent the purist temples discussing the value of the organization's work. Police watched and listened, but building a case against any purist for expressing an opinion had little success. No one doubted that radicalization was taking place. But as long as the conversations focused on religious theory and remained in the temples, the police had their hands tied.

As the debates and national attention grew, Alice and David continued to work. The lab work was difficult enough; but on top of that, they had agreed to occasional news interviews at the urging of Mr. Germond and the team of PR specialists at Dresden Industries. The company needed to keep a positive light on what it was doing, and letting the public hear directly from the lead geneticists was the best way they knew to accomplish that.

The media however, had bestowed the two scientists with new names that only increased the number of viewers, opinions, and scrutiny. They became known as The Creators. While gypsies showed indifference and calcunists paid little attention other than to express a tingle of pride that their faith had been given two honorary religious icons, purists were far less passive.

From the moment the title first aired, it was replicated almost instantly throughout the press. Internet searches for the word 'creator' now brought up articles on The Quiet One as well as featured stories, biographies, and publications of David Allens and Alice Clarke. Articles comparing The Quiet One's creation with that of the two creators were now prominent across discussion boards. The comments were some of praise exalting the progress of science while others were outspokenly hostile threatening revenge by believers of the true creation and by The Quiet One Herself. The attention was too much to bear, and the two scientists retreated into the lab as much as possible.

In the midst of a whirlwind of exposure growing daily around the two geneticists, Martha Clarke ventured to the city and met with her daughter for lunch. Alice sat across the table eyeing the woman who had always been a source of inspiration and intimidation.

In her early sixties, Martha had no concept of age other than its ability to be manipulated. Her skin was almost without a single wrinkle. Alice knew the skin shedding serum had always been a favorite of her mothers. It was obvious the woman was a frequent member of the clinics. Her soft brown hair with reddish tints fell just below the shoulders. When she smiled, it always gave away her social awareness that she was speaking with someone who never quite matched her caliber. Alice knew this last part well and did her best not to cower when it appeared.

"You really have been making quite the name for yourself," Martha told her daughter before taking another sip of white wine. She closed her eyes and savored the delicate earthy balance then smiled with approval. "I remember when it was my name shouted from the rooftops. But just yesterday I read an article where I was referred to as the creator's mother." She threw her head back in a moment of laughter that was more theatrical than genuine.

As soon as Alice accepted her mother's invitation for lunch, she had known how the event would play out. This was only the beginning. For as far back as the woman could remember, her mother had always had a talent for directing the conversation onto herself. They would discuss the weather, and Martha would feign concern that Alice was spending too much time in the sun only as a prelude to mentioning her new summer hat. Alice's top marks on university exams were a reason for her mother to reminisce about her own school days and how far she had come since then. In fact, even Alice's employment at Dresden Industries had been single-handedly brought about because of Martha's recommendation, a fact that would never be forgotten.

"At first, I was a bit upset at losing my own identity and only being known as your mother, that is until I finished the article and found that the journalist more than made up for it by concluding that genius is hereditary. He even provided a small list of my more well-known accomplishments on the side just to prove that the apple really didn't fall far from the tree. I'm so proud of you, darling. And if your father were still alive, I'm certain he would be just as pleased at what he and I were able to create."

There it was. Alice kept the fake smile on her face while the words rang in her ears like nails on a chalkboard. She had made a name for herself at Dresden Industries; but for her mother, any success on Alice's part would be another medal to hang around her own neck. She took a sip of the dirty martini knowing any argument was pointless.

"Thanks mom, but I can hardly take all the credit. I've never worked with someone like David. He's brilliant in a way I never thought possible. We make a really good team."

"Doctor David Allens," she said with a nod. "He's quite the figure himself. When you initially told me you two were paired together, I took some time to look up his qualifications. And I must say, some of his earlier work reminded me of myself at a younger age."

"I think he could give even you a run for your money," Alice mumbled knowing full well such a comment was bound to get under her mother's skin.

"Hardly," Martha dismissed the outrageous idea with the wave of a hand. "He's certainly creative, but there's a certain amount of experience that even he still stands to learn. It wouldn't be easy, but in time I have no doubt Dr. Allens could be one of the greats."

"You've read the news," Alice said beginning to feel a bit uncomfortable with the direction of this conversation. "He's already well on that track."

"Darling," Mrs. Clarke said with sudden seriousness. "Now isn't the time to mess around and hope for the best. What this project entails affects the entire world. Something that important requires ingenuity, genius, creativity, and most of all, experience to keep things on the right track."

Alice sat back in her chair suddenly aware of why her mother had extended the lunch invitation and what this meeting was really about. Her stomach turned at the thought. She would never live up to her mother's standards. And equally hurtful, Martha would never consider her an equal within the scientific community. The room spun as Alice predicted what was to happen next.

"We're on the right track, mother," Alice said in a futile last defense.

"I've already spoken to the board at Dresden Industries, and they've agreed that a change in project leadership is in order. They want someone who already has a name with the experience to match. It would go so much better with the public considering all the controversy surrounding things lately."

"You're taking our project away from us?"

"This isn't about you. This is about what's best to get us all to the finish line. When I first wrote that recommendation, I had no idea they would be pairing you up with Dr. Allens. I have no doubt he's been instrumental in every aspect of the gene development. But you might've bitten off more than you can chew, and he can't very well reach his full potential and carry you at the same time. He needs a partner that can match him in every aspect.

"Please don't feel bad. I felt terrible enough for the both of us the moment I learned you two were working together. I always wanted the best for you, but I didn't know getting you hired was going to accentuate your shortcomings..."

Alice couldn't speak. She couldn't move. Over a single martini, her life had been turned upside down. It wasn't enough that the woman was a creator's mother, she needed to be The Quiet One Herself! If growing up around such an icon had taught Alice anything, it was that being the daughter of the famous Martha Clarke meant she only carried half the genes for success. The other half were never of much importance.

"...We of course want the original team to save face and will keep you on," Alice half-heard her mother say. "I'm not as young as I used to be and will need an assistant to help me with all the tedious tasks. And as soon as Dr. Allens gives his consent, the board will make the transition that very day."

Her ears suddenly perked, and Alice snapped back into the present. "The board needs David's consent?"

"They're only formalities really," Martha said again wiping away the details as mundane. "The board actually requires the consent from both lead geneticists. But after I explained to them your desire to work with someone of my standing and be done with those horrid news interviews, they understand Dr. Allen's consent is all they're waiting on at this point."

The world was spinning. She hadn't lost her job, not yet anyway. She wasn't being pushed out. If she chose, Alice would be giving it away to someone overly qualified. She felt tears beneath the surface and tried to control her breathing. How could she? Her own mother....

"The board never contacted you. You contacted them. Didn't you?"

"This is a matter of faith," the woman said suddenly trying a different approach. "When I heard what was happening, I knew I was meant to be a part of it. I brought you up to be a calcunist who always puts the faith above all else. I would think that part of you would be grateful for the opportunity to see progress make such a leap and to give it the best chance for success."

"My religion is important to me, but I don't see how handing over my life's work is going to add any more meaning to my life. Right now, I'm practicing what it preaches. You can't ask any more from anyone."

"But that's my point," Alice's mother said leaning a little closer. "You've already done as much as you're able. No one is doubting you're giving it everything you have, but maybe that's not enough. I know this isn't easy to accept, but think about what you're striving for. If someone is going to be given the name creator, they must live up to that title." She reached for Alice's hand. "Being the daughter of the creator will still do wonders for your reputation. You'll still matter."

Alice pulled her hand away as two silent tears ran down her cheeks. Her face was flushed. She smelled those loathsome honeysuckles and suddenly couldn't figure out if they were coming from herself or from Martha. This is what it had come down to. Decades of pent up frustration at never being good enough had finally peaked in a moment of absolute hatred for the woman across the table.

She wanted to scream out every fowl thought this woman had made her feel for so long. As any therapist would surely point out, getting it off her chest could only be for the best. But for some reason, her eyes drifted down to the empty martini glass in front of her. The shouting would have to wait. For now, she sat there quietly before slowly rising to her feet.

"As the creator's mother, you still matter." And with that, Alice kept her head low as she silently turned and walked away.

THIRTEEN

It's a beautiful thing to share thoughts and feelings with someone close. For some, it makes all the difference in the world. The burden of life's problems is lessened, and two people grow closer as a result. But with Alice, getting the words out was as difficult as she imagined.

She and David had grown closer over the last few months. And as a sign of trust, she didn't want to keep such a big secret to herself. She knew David would support her. She knew that the science they had completed so far would speak for itself and prove the need for their continued partnership through the entire process. But at the same time, she was afraid.

Logic and reason seldom play a role when emotion sweeps them out the window. Alice found herself wondering if the opportunity to work with the renowned Martha Clarke would be far too tempting for David to resist. After all, every geneticist strives to be the best, and maybe her mother was right to think that she was barely keeping up. It was an illogical fear, but it still remained.

Though she never thought about the momentary vexation on the first day she and David met, it came back to her as justification for her fears. When they had been brainstorming ideas, he had made a comment about working with her mother. Granted, they had both shrugged it off as nothing more than nonsense. But he had still said it. Alice couldn't help but wonder if her David really held that desire somewhere deep inside.

Her eyes had become moist during the metro ride home. And with the dread of revealing all to David, she was an anxious mess. The familiar and despised honeysuckle odor came off of her with each nervous thought. And when she walked in the door, Alice wished she had changed her genetic sequencing on the day that smell first appeared.

With so much panic, what Alice hadn't been expecting was the man's calm disposition. She rehashed the dreadful lunch with her mother all the while watching David's face. Obviously, a lot must be going on in that head; but for all Alice could see, he could still win at any hand of cards.

"Say something," she finally said at last. His silence had become too much for her to bear. She wasn't foolish enough to think such an opportunity wasn't in his best interest. And if that's what he decided, then she needed to brace herself and be ready to leave the room. As much as she loved him, being replaced by her mother even in the workplace still didn't sit well.

"So your mother is ready to start immediately?" He asked.

Alice's head lowered. She knew something like this would happen. With everything going so well, it was foolish to think some downfall wasn't on the horizon. And it finally arrived. "Yes," she said at last. "She's ready to start right away. As soon as we sign the consent forms, she'll move into the lab."

Knowing this was what David wanted, she decided then and there to give her consent at the first possible chance. As much as she felt betrayed, Alice wasn't about to make waves and possibly ruin her chances to continue working at Dresden Industries - but in a different area. There was no way she could continue to see his face every day and be something less in his eyes.

"That's bold," David continued. "We've been at it for seven months now, and your mother thinks she'd be ready to take over without so much as even reviewing our notes first?"

"She'll catch up in no time. Listen," Alice said feeling her voice beginning to falter and rising from her seat. "I have to run some errands before it gets too late." There was no doubt this meant the end of their relationship. She tried to hold back the tears and walked to the door.

"Wait," David said rising and looking around a little uncomfortably. "Don't I get a say in this?"

Alice stopped in her tracks. There was no reason to hide her look of surprise. It was plain as day. What more of a say could he possibly have? Did he feel the need to give her an explanation? Standing there and listening was asking too much of her.

"It's fine," she said brushing the question away with the wave of her hand. "I'll see you back in the lab tomorrow." Of course she wouldn't. She would clear out her stuff when no one was around. But David didn't need to know that right now.

"You may be willing to sign away our partnership so easily, but I'm not," David said bluntly. Alice looked back to see him standing there agitated and nervous. She knew him well enough to know taking such a bold stance against her wasn't something he enjoyed, and doing so now obviously was making him apprehensive.

"What?" She asked as if the words had been completely foreign to her.

"I won't do it," he said flatly. "I know how important this project is, but we started it together and should finish it that way. We work well together - in and out of the lab. Why should we change something that's producing such good results?"

Alice had been a walking personification of stress; but when she realized David was trying his best to convince her to stay on with him, she couldn't help but laugh. In less than thirty seconds, her life and career had gone from disaster to the way it was that morning. A flood of relief swept over her, but she still needed to hear him say it outright. His comment from ages ago about the famous Martha Clarke was still fresh in her mind.

"So you don't want to work with my mother?" She asked putting the question out there so there would be no misunderstandings.

"Of course not. We're in this together. Please don't walk away."

With outstretched arms, Alice walked across the room and closed the distance between them. In less than a second, she was holding David and had no intention of letting him go. Confession after confession poured from her lips into the man's ear until at last she understood that it had been her own fear of inadequacies that had made her think the worst.

"Your mother may also smell like honeysuckles," David said with a grin. "But she's not you. And besides, creators aren't replaced that easily."

FOURTEEN

Mr. Germond sat alone in his office staring out the window. As head of the research division at Dresden Industries, he was the man in charge. Surely he should have all the answers. But in this instance, he was at a loss.

The Horsemen was making more than just a nuisance of itself. Two synchronized attacks on vaccine production facilities had left behind nothing but piles of rubble. Fortunately, the buildings had been empty. But the equipment and supplies - all ruined. To make matters worse, there was no way the company could fulfill its orders for the next three months. With one factory down, it could still get by with partial shortages across the board. But with two factories out of commission, the effects were catastrophic.

Thankfully, Mr. Germond was not in charge of cleaning up that mess. But since a spray-painted message left behind at the scene of what had once been a state-of-the-art facility had singled out the research division, he had to get ahead of this thing. 'Creating without conscience is declaring war on The Quiet One,' is what the pavement read. And blowing around across the debris were pages upon pages of one thing: the announcement of the next step of human evolution and its anticipated completion date. Someone had littered them far and wide making sure the message was loud and clear.

"Come in," Mr. Germond said solemnly as Martin poked his head in the door.

"You wanted to see me?" His assistant asked carrying a tablet in case taking notes and rescheduling meetings or press conferences were in order.

"Close the door, Martin," he said taking one final glance out the window before turning his attention on his assistant. "Are you up to speed with last night's attack?"

"I heard it on the news on the way in this morning," the man told him. "Not exactly the best way to start the day."

"It certainly isn't," Mr. Germond agreed. "I'm getting all the same news as everyone else about this Horsemen group and can't seem to make heads or tails of it. It seems everything that has something to do with science if fair game in their eyes. And since it looks like our human development project is the next target, I could use a purist's point of view to help with security. Any news in the temples?

Martin wasn't surprised by this question. Openly a purist but with no quarrels with progress or religious differences, he had offered to be Mr. Germond's eyes and ears on more than one occasion. Far be it to be seen as a spy, but the man's conscious gave him no choice. Purism, as he saw it, required him to act in the service of The Quiet One. He could think of no better way to do this than to save all manners of creation. Though some were further along than others, surely all things had stemmed from The Quiet One's very womb. And as such, all things should be saved.

"There are more sympathizers with The Horsemen every day in the temples," Martin told him. "Sometimes, it's hard to know which way people are leaning unless they start talking about the purist cause.

"As for security, I would warn you to be cautious of all age groups and sexes. At first I thought The Horsemen was a bunch of middle-aged men, but more and more I've been hearing young and old people of all sorts talking about them. My godson occasionally tells me stories of rubbing shoulders with a few of them. And if youth are involved in the attacks, it's likely to assume that the plans will become more dramatic and even careless."

"How is Gregory?" the director asked curiously.

"He's well. I hear he's in between jobs at the moment, but I have no doubt he'll find something without much trouble."

"Well, if what you say is true," Mr. Germond said calmly returning to the subject at hand. "That would certainly account for the vaccine facilities. It was only half thought out."

"What do you mean?"

"The attacks created a shortage of vaccines," Mr. Germond began. "I suppose that was their intention. But I would've assumed they had given any thought as to how Dresden Industries is to deal with the shortage when we still have to fulfill our quota."

"Won't Dresden fall behind until we can get a new building up and running?" Martin asked.

Mr. Germond looked out the window deep in thought. The events of last night had certainly taken a toll on him, but he tried to keep that to himself.

"Under normal circumstances, it would take months to fix this mess with a new facility. And then there's the issue of the human development project being a target. It's only a matter of time before that group finds a way to sabotage the project or the entire building." He took a deep breath and looked at Martin intently. "I need to ask you what the purist community would think if 1 moved the project's timetable ahead of schedule."

"For those that aren't sympathetic to The Horsemen," Martin said plainly. "I don't think they'll have much of an opinion whether it takes two months or three before they see a new product out there. But are you sure that's wise considering the rest of the mess the attacks are creating?"

"That's why I'm considering it. I haven't run it by the board yet, but I'm fairly confident they'll be thrilled at the notion. I needed your thoughts on the matter first. Since we still need to fill the order for vaccines but don't have any left, I can use the human development project to kill two birds with one stone. Releasing the serum to the public will fulfill our government order, and at the same time we'll get the project out of the lab before the radicals have the chance to plan another attack."

"The Horsemen may view the updated timetable as a way to thwart their efforts," Martin told him.

Mr. Germond nodded in agreement. "I certainly do hope it has that effect. But they really should've known we would do everything we could to cope with this disaster. Attacks like these really should be given much more careful thought.

FIFTEEN

The table felt cold to the touch. David wondered if every news guest brought to the station thought the same thing. It was made of glass and blended in well with the many illuminated screens behind him. But still so cold. He had once used a desk just like it nearly a decade ago, but even then the man remembered how much he had disliked it. Impossible to keep clean and with every little fingerprint leaving a smudge, it had always made him feel like the dirtiest person on the planet.

As soon as word spread that the human development project was being released ahead of schedule, phones began ringing off the hook. Everyone wanted the story. It wasn't enough that

David and Alice had already been covered on every news outlet for months now, the journalists wanted more.

To his relief, David was thrilled when Mr. Germond conferred with him and Alice about the new release date. It meant an increase in lab hours which in turn meant a decrease in public appearances and interviews. Both he and Alice didn't mind this in the least. They preferred having the extra time to themselves.

But with the announcement of the new date, one more news interview was in order. There was no way to avoid it. Though reporters tried to negotiate ten interviews that would be a series and give each news anchor a chance to carry the torch, Mr. Germond approved a single interview for either David or Alice to attend at their convenience. But then it was back to the lab and thereby ending things on a positive note.

David sat in front of the cameras while a man with salt and pepper hair thanked him for the time before launching into questions about the project. The reporter repeated almost everything

David said. It was vexing to say the least, but the way the man tried to make a connection with the camera and his audience let David know which focal point he really preferred on the television.

"Let me ask you," the man said while leaning forward in his chair. "You've been called a creator. People of all religions are comparing you and your partner to The Quiet One. That's an enormous role and responsibility to fill. How are you planning to accomplish this?"

"As I'm sure you're aware, the media was the first to give us that reputation," David said and watched as the man's mouth gave a slight twitch. "In genetics, we do create since that's what the job requires. But to compare us with an all-powerful deity from long ago before time itself existed is as ridiculous as thinking Dr. Clarke and myself could ever fulfill such a role. We're simply working to help mankind progress. And as geneticists, we've identified several ways to use our knowledge and resources to accomplish this."

"You're working to help mankind progress," the man repeated with an air of importance. "And this progress will carry us away from, and I quote," he said glancing down at his notes, "...a flaw in the design." He waited for a reaction from David that, much to his secret disappointment, never came.

"That's correct," David said as if the two were discussing the weather.

"This flaw," he continued sensing his audience's need for sensationalism instead of mere facts. "Do you blame The Quiet One herself for this flawed design?"

The news studio was silent aside from the sound of a porcelain cup falling to the floor and breaking into pieces. All eyes were on the pair. For a long moment, David remained silent looking at the man who in turn looked back at him with a sense of victory. A question had been asked that would incite outrage no matter the answer. A publicist from Dresden Industries was in the control booth with arms flying in the air. No doubt she was demanding the sly journalist be fired on the spot. But at that moment during a live broadcast, there was nothing to be done but answer.

"Could you repeat the question?" David asked returning his focus on the man.

"I'd be happy to," and David believed he was actually telling the truth. "Do you blame The Quiet One for the flaw we know as mankind?"

"The answer depends on whether you believe misery is what makes mankind all that it is."

"So you blame The Quiet One for mankind's misery?"

It took all of David's effort to keep his face from showing concern. The man was twisting his words; and if he succeeded, David would be known as the one alienating an entire religious group within society. He needed to choose his words carefully, but it was difficult to do so against a man with a seasoned tongue.

"To say that a design flaw is a reason for personal animosity or a grudge against The Quiet One is simply untrue."

"But nevertheless," the journalist continued without missing a beat. "You and your partner do believe that you can update creation and fix those flaws. Might this be some kind of rivalry between creators to see which one can ultimately do better?"

What was there to say? How ever David tried to deflect the question, he knew the man would only find a way to spin his answer into something else. Was this an interview or a set up? He had to get ahead of this, but there was no way as long as that egotist in a suit continued to ask the questions.

David knew he couldn't stall forever. The longer he waited, the more talk there was out there in the world. Every viewer was watching his silence and interpreting it in some way. And for what David knew about society, he was certain they weren't willing to give him the benefit of the doubt.

The journalist was waiting for David's answer. Leaning forward with anticipation, he could practically see his prey squirming under his grip. A few more questions would be all it took to finish what he had started. He gave the camera a brief smile to show that he wasn't affected by the secrets being divulged by his guest.

"Do you have any children?" David asked suddenly, and the man with salt and pepper hair was taken aback.

"That's quite the way to change the subject," he commented brushing a hand through his carefully combed hair. "But I believe our viewers are waiting to know about this rivalry you have with The Quiet One."

"And I'll answer that question as soon as you answer mine," David shot back just as quickly with a smile. "The two go hand in hand, you see. I wouldn't dream of changing the subject. But I have to ask you this question in order to give you my answer."

The man sat back in his chair eyeing his prey. Whatever his guest had in mind, it was peculiar. But the only question on the journalist's head was whether he had the skill to turn the conversation back around as soon as this nonsense was done with. It was certainly uncomfortable not knowing in which direction the guest's answer would take, but he rose above it.

"Alright then," he said turning his eyes to the camera to show the ludicrously of the situation. "Yes, I have one child, a five-year-old boy."

"What 's he like?"

"He's like most children his age" he said with another twitch of his mouth. "Determined, curious, and a natural born explorer. But that's enough about him. Let's continue with..."

"That's my point exactly," David interrupted before the man could finish. "As a parent, you want to encourage those qualities and see how he develops. He has so much potential, and you wouldn't dream of keeping him locked in his room where he couldn't develop."

"I most certainly would not," he agreed with an eye at the camera showing the audience his human side.

"But like so many other children, he will have certain disadvantages in life. He's still susceptible to diseases like chicken pox. Unless he's one of the fortunate few who were vaccinated before the attacks last month?"

The man nodded. "He's been vaccinated already."

"I'm certainly glad to hear that," David continued without missing a beat. "But what about other diseases that will require vaccinations when he's six or seven? What happens if he breaks a bone because he's playing a little too rough? Years down the line, what happens if he wants to do more with life but can't because of bad joints or poor blood circulation to the limbs?"

"As you know already, doctor, there are procedures and serums in place to keep him in perfect working order."

"Now to answer your question," David said at last. "Because my partner and I have an appreciation for creation as it is, we do not have a rivalry or grudge against anything that could create so many things that we enjoy. But as geneticists, we have learned to improve on the foundation that has already been laid. We can fix your son's broken bones and vaccinate him against diseases for the next century. But to give him the best chance at reaching his full potential, we've developed a way to strengthen his body and do away with most common diseases altogether. Surely as a parent who keeps your child vaccinated, you'd rather he receives one serum that will let him live a better life than twenty vaccinations that will have to be renewed intermittently."

"If you choose to play the part of The Quiet One, people will not take that lying down," the man said at last knowing his original plan was no more.

"If I chose to be The Quiet One," David replied as he watched a group of police officers silently enter the studio. "I would make a poor substitute. She and I have very different opinions on life. Unlike Her, I live in this world. And as a calcunist, it's my responsibility to find ways to improve the parts of the world that need it. That's what I'm doing for your son and everyone. And with the human development project, it'll be much more effective."

The producer was only too relieved to call a break and bring an end to the interview. As soon as the cameras were off, the police stepped in. Though the journalist insisted he was only after the truth,

the police had already confirmed the interview to be a potential act of inciting radicalization and violence against calcunist practices. Arrested and escorted out of the studio, his tongue continued to try its tricks. But by now, no one cared to listen.

SIXTEEN

Weeks passed as the human development promotions continued to build. There was little time for the world to catch up to speed with progress, but the media did its best to accomplish the task. The Horsemen continued its own anti-progress movement that rallied supporters online and through secret meetings. No one could say for certain to what extent the organization had grown, but everyone kept an eye out for any sign of The Horsemen's personal brand of violence.

When the day finally came to release the project to the public, David and Alice heard the first explosions from his apartment. The entire building vibrated from the impact. Looking at each other with alarm, they immediately jumped out of bed and ran to the window. Both had tried to keep a positive face but inwardly were concerned that something like this might happen. And as soon as they heard the sound from the first blast, each knew it was as they feared.

The quiet between blasts was horrific. From what they could see, piles of dark smoke rose in two different locations. Boom boom boom. Then a third. Boom boom boom. Then a fourth. They could hear neighbors screaming, but it took what felt like an eternity before the sound of sirens came moving through the city somewhere in the distance.

Milo sat on Alice's lap while she and David glued their eyes to the television. Reports were still coming in. In total, twelve of the fifteen medical clinics were reduced to rubble. Doctors and serum facilitators had arrived early to make preparations for the growing lines of eager customers waiting just outside. The casualties were severe, and even many in line fell victim to the blasts.

"Instead of leaving the usual anti-progress message as is their custom," the newsman told his salivating audience on the other side of the television screen. "The Horsemen has contacted the newsroom directly and left a message. To be clear," he said picking up a piece of paper with trembling hands and addressing the camera. "These words come directly from The Horsemen. I am in no way condoning the group's behavior or supporting its message. This is not an attempt to radicalize but merely to offer you, our audience, The Horsemen's explanation for why it committed this horrendous act." His eyes lowered as he began to read.

We, as a people, are all from the same origin. Creation has made us, and we owe our very existence to The Quiet One. She chose to give us life and the world as it once was. That was perfection in all its glory.

That day has long since passed. What we have now is something innovative but less than perfect in every way. We have forced ourselves to settle for less than we truly are. Because of this, we have lost sight of our true purpose and existence.

Altering what The Quiet One has made so perfectly is nothing less than an act of aggression. Because of our tolerance of calcunists and their religious practices, we as a people have suffered. No longer will this be the case. We will no longer tolerate the birth of abominations and stand idly by while The Quiet One weeps for her creations. This is our position, and we are ready to act in creations' best interest.

The journalist put down the sheet of paper and took a moment for the words to sink in with his viewers. His hands delicately rested on top of the paper. But even then, he noticed their placement and tried to carefully remove them as if in hopes of removing himself from everything that the single sheet of paper represented.

His words trailed on while suddenly David and Alice's phones began to ring simultaneously. Without waiting for the smoke to settle, the news hoped the creators would have a response to The Horsemen's attacks as well as the group's statement. The speed was shocking, but not surprising. After all, would the press be able to say it was doing its job if the greatest opposition hadn't at least been asked for a quick comment?

While Alice politely referred them to the publicity department at Dresden Industries, David had less luck getting rid of the reporter on the other end of his line.

"C'mon," the voice insisted. "You've lived through this once already and barely made it out alive the first time. Now that The Horsemen is back at it, how does that make you feel?"

Although it was a complete stranger asking the questions, David's sentiments were still the same. He was alive by blind luck as he already knew quite well. His eye could see perfectly, but it would never be exactly the same. Bringing up these old memories threatened to spark something inside that the man wasn't sure he could control. He tried again to get rid of the reporter.

"What if it had been Dr. Clarke working in one of those clinics this morning. How would something like that affect a fellow creator?"

"It would be the end of perfection," he said before his mind had time to catch up. Before he had time to explain, the reporter thanked him for his time and hung up to make the front-page headline. David stood there holding the dead phone in the air with eyes closed. He wasn't sure what damage had been caused, but he was certain he'd have the answer in a matter of hours. The media was good about spreading the word, and this was yet another story to tell. His hand drooped, and the phone didn't dare disturb the silence.

"I hope that comment was in response to The Horsemen," Alice said with a smile after she hung up on her line. "But I'm not sure if that group will actually bring about the end of perfection. It'll destroy a lot in the process, but there's bound to be some perfect things left."

"I wasn't talking about them," David confessed as his eyes opened before what he knew would be the coming storm. "The reporter asked me what would happen if it were you in the bombings. ...I didn't know what to say. It came out without even thinking."

"You think it would be the end of perfection if I was gone?" She asked with a sympathetic smile on her face that wanted to cover David in kisses for having such a sweet thought. "It's a bit morbid, but I'm flattered all the same."

David would've been happy to shrug off the comment as a romantic's silly outlook on life if that's all it was, but something inside told him that no one would let it rest at that. He wiped it away with a smile all the while hoping that would be the end of it, but his heart sank when his comment was repeated only twenty minutes later on television.

"If I have this right," a newsman in glasses said while discussing various events with a discussion panel. "When confronted with the potential death of his fellow creator, Dr. Allens was quoted as saying 'It would be the end of perfection.' We all know the two spend quite a bit of time together with the human development project, and it would be reasonable to assume he's sentimental towards his partner. Wouldn't you all agree?"

"I'm afraid I wholeheartedly disagree," a woman replied on the panel beside two men who nodded frivolously. "If we were to think of him as just an ordinary man, then yes, that would make sense. But let's not kid ourselves. He's no more ordinary than I am to mastering the secrets of the universe overnight in my sleep. There's a reason we call him a creator. And after the attacks to keep his evolutionary creations off the streets, there's no doubt that his comment was directed at The Horsemen."

"And what did it mean?" The man in glasses asked while scanning the faces of his conversationalists for an answer.

"It's quite clear, isn't it?" A heavyset man said adamantly. "Because of what's been accomplished, there is a new order to things. A new level of perfection has been reached that we can all attain at the clinics. But the mind is something that has not been touched. And the destruction of something so precious as that of a creator's mind is beyond unthinkable - it's monstrous. We know as a calcunist he would never take progress off the market, but it is worth questioning whether that progress will keep its current form if something were to happen to one of the only two living creators in existence."

"Are you suggesting the human development serum might now be unsafe? That's preposterous! Nothing in its composition has changed since yesterday. And if there was any tampering, you could rest assured The Horsemen is the one responsible."

"So the end of perfection was Dr. Allens' way of setting the truth ablaze as it were," the man in glasses clarified. "The death of a creator has significant repercussions, and it was partially a plea to The Horsemen not to cross that line. Perfection will be altered in some way; and if that group is not careful, it will inadvertently unleash the wrath of a creator on the world."

David sat next to Alice watching the discussion unfold. He had known his comment had the makings of an avalanche, and the destruction had only begun. He looked at Alice and tried to explain himself. But every time he opened his mouth, the words would disappear. For all of his intellect, there was no way of making sense of what the experts were saying. Instead, he took Alice's hand and hoped she understood.

"Now what we have here," the news voices continued delving deeper into the storm, "is a textbook example of purism versus progress. In the old days, it was the calcunists who sought progress at the expense of devout belief in The Quiet One. She had lost that battle, and Her creations were changed. Now if we skip forward to the present, we find that the tables have completely shifted. It's the calcunists and their religious pursuit for progress that's at stake while purist radicals will stop at nothing to return all faith to the prior."

"So both instances are battles of fundamentalist groups versus creators."

"That's precisely right," the man went on. "But this time, The Creators will not roll over so easily. And if a group like The Horsemen is adamant to wage war against designers of creation themselves, then we should all be prepared to take a side."

"Do you really think it will come to that?" A panel member asked. "Let me remind you that so far, the violence has only been from one side. The Creators have not sought vengeance and have been letting law enforcement take care of the matter."

"It would be foolish on my part to speak for a creator," the man went on. "But there's no doubt from Doctor Allens' comment that further violence will not continue to be tolerated. And when that moment comes, I certainly don't want to be among the guilty party seeing The Creators' wrath firsthand. Whether we are calcunists, purists, or gypsies, we're all either on the side of perfection or against it. Let me remind you that The Quiet One loves all of Her creations and would be adamantly against any of its destruction no matter how updated or altered it has become. To say that She approves of murder in any form goes against Her very nature which we all know is love, and it truly is a crime that a group claiming to act in Her name is willing to strip away the decency of the purist faith."

"Are you suggesting that, according to the purist belief, our calcunist creators have deviated away from the time of the original creation but are still acting in The Quiet One's best interest by keeping Her creations alive?"

"I couldn't agree with you more," the woman said enthusiastically. "They aren't purists, and it would be ridiculous to think they would govern life by that standard. But they do seem to possess an underlying protection of all creation in everything they've strived to achieve. For the sake of showing uniformity for those who create, it's better to think of our calcunist creators and The Quiet One as equals in their love for all life. In that regard, our world consists of three creators of equal importance rather than focusing on their differences. And if there are to be battle lines drawn as my companion here suggests, then the only question worth asking is whether or not we each stand with The Creators or oppose them..."

Alice tried to keep her jaw from dropping, but some things felt like they were beyond her control. And hearing the news authority's view on things, keeping her mouth shut felt utterly impossible.

The memory of her mother's words rang in her ears, and Alice wondered if the diva had been right to spot the need for a more experienced voice to be a Creator. She tried to brush the thought away as quickly as it had come, but the words from the television gave her the urge to scream for help - and who better to call to than a parent? She chastised herself knowing sympathy was not the emotion Martha was best known for.

The mood was grim in the apartment. Neither one knew how to handle what they were hearing. It was Milo who made the first sound, and then he couldn't stop. It was laughter – pure unadulterated laughter. Even for a dog, he couldn't believe what he was hearing. With so many formulated opinions coming across as facts by the newsgroup, his laughter reached new heights.

"You're starting a war for all of creation!" He howled uncontrollably. "Are you going to be as bloodthirsty as they're making you out to be?"

"You know it's not true, right?" Alice asked. "I'm sure Dresden Industries is already on top of this. They'll know what to do."

"I wouldn't count on it," Milo said in between fits of laughter. "They haven't mentioned Dresden Industries once," the dog reminded them. "The public only wants to hear from The Creators at this point."

Neither David nor Alice wanted to acknowledge this point, but deep inside both knew it to be true. Somewhere between speeding up the release of human development and its release, The Creators had outgrown their mechanism for delivery. It didn't matter that Mr. Germond was still the manager behind the science of progress - David and Alice were now associated with progress as faith. They had a following, and the world watched to see how divinity came into existence.

"We've just gotten word that the three remaining clinics have successfully delivered the serum to twelve thousand in the city before they ran out of supplies," the news reporter announced later that evening. "In response to the attacks, Dresden Industries said it is shocked and horrified that The Horsemen would take away life so indifferently. But nevertheless, it will not compromise its human obligation. That's why thirteen government buildings have been transformed into temporary clinic sites and will be up and running by tomorrow. Full security measures will be in effect guaranteeing the public's safety. And because the reserve serum is housed in an undisclosed location, it will still be possible to administer the serum to the city's entire population by the end of the week."

The phones rang yet again. By now, David and Alice had ·stopped counting. They merely picked up, referred the press to Dresden Industries, and hung up without waiting for a response. This would've been yet another monotone monologue if Calvin's voice had not interrupted David halfway through.

"Did you hear the news?" Calvin asked excitedly. "We're going to win this after all!"

David tried to keep his voice calm and rubbed his temples. "Win what? If you've been listening to the news, none of it's true."

"You mean you and Alice aren't behind the battle for all mankind? That's unfortunate. It would've been a thrill to fight alongside The Creators."

Milo let out a laugh that was muffled in his paw. David flashed him an irritable look.

"I know you and Alice aren't really the fighting types," he continued over the receiver. "But there's more than a few taking it seriously." People were shouting in the background, and he covered the phone with his hand until it passed.

"Where are you?" David asked.

"I'm where you should be right now," Calvin told him with a smile that came across even over the distance. "There's a few siding against you two, but the majority are clearly standing by you. I'm with the latter. We have a demonstration going on right in front of Dresden Industries. If you and Alice are in the middle of something, hurry it up and get over here. You both need to see this."

SEVENTEEN

It was nearly midnight by the time Alice and David exited the metro station and climbed the stairs to see Dresden Industries standing like a beacon. For such a late night, the station was filled with lingerers and late-night passersby wanting to take in a glimpse of the scene. The world was alive. And above the many metro lines that ran underground, the streets were filled.

There was shouting, laughter and singing from the streets. All were in a merry mood for some unspoken reason that seemed to bring all of humanity together. But as soon as the first spectators caught sight of the two Creators ascending the metro steps, whispers began to erupt from all areas of the crowd.

At first it was a fleeting glance that perhaps this young couple holding hands was out for a late-night stroll and like so many others had been drawn in to see what all the commotion was about. But a second glance was all it took for the masses to recognize the faces that had lived on every news outlet for months now. There were whispers, fingers pointing in their direction, and finally smiles of exultation as many felt blessed to be in the presence of gods.

Cheers erupted from every direction. The scene felt outrageous as neither one knew how to handle such a following. All they could do was continue walking and smile at the many faces that looked to them for a sign of something otherworldly. David wished he had followed his first instinct and stayed home.

Amid the cheers and hollers, Calvin emerged from the crowd instantly giving David a feeling of relief. Finally, someone who knew what was happening could get him and Alice out of there.

Calvin led the pair forward until they found themselves standing in front of Dresden Industries. The crowd was keeping its distance, and it was only then that Alice noticed the smile spread across Calvin's face.

"Calvin," she said as if addressing one of David's friends whom she tolerated on occasion. "What's going on?"

"They're waiting for you to say something," he said looking from one face to the other. "Look, after what happened today with those Horsemen, the people need to rally behind something; and since you represent their future, it might as well be you two."

"That pregnant woman looks like she's planning to name her firstborn after me," David said eyeing a woman in the crowd. "I really don't think we should be encouraging these people."

"I agree," Alice said at once. "Coming here was a bad idea."

"But look at the lives you're affecting," Calvin continued. "You'll always be a couple of lab geeks to me, but that doesn't change the fact that you've earned the right to be called Creators. That means something. And whether or not you choose to believe it, these people do. Let them find faith where they can just like you both do."

David knew his friend well enough to know the man wasn't about to back down. And the more he looked at the crowd, the more he understood. Some displayed full heads of hair while others wore hats. For the first time that night, he noticed that those present contained gypsies, calcunists, and even purists. All were here in support of creation, and it made sense that such a simple sentiment would bring all three of the faiths together.

"We have to say something," David told Alice at last.

"Are you crazy? You saw the news. They're planning for us to lead them in to battle."

"We have to say something," David repeated.

"You'll be doing the talking," she countered. "I'm no good at public speaking without my notes."

"You heard her," Calvin said giving his friend a pat on the back. "They're all yours."

David's mouth suddenly became dry as he raised his hands to silence the crowd. They responded almost immediately, and he was left with the eyes of thousands staring at him with his hands still in the air. He put them down.

"I don't have anything prepared," he said as loudly as he could. "But I'll be happy to answer your questions. Does anybody have one?"

Instantaneously, hands flew up from all over. And much to his delight, the masses were patient as he pointed to one.

"What are you planning to do about The Horsemen?" a man asked with hopeful eyes.

"You don't start with the small things, do you?" David said and tried to think of something clever while the audience chuckled to itself. But the more he thought, the more nothing came to mind. He looked at Alice for support. She gave him an encouraging smile that seemed to say, you're in an impossible situation. Do your best.

"I don't know what can be done against a group whose only objective is it blow things up, but we're certainly not planning to go to war against them."

"But don't they threaten everything you're trying to accomplish?" Someone asked.

David nodded. "I think the attacks today were clear evidence of that. But that's for law enforcement to handle." He paused and thought for a moment before adding. "And once the police have bettered themselves through the human development serum, they'll be able to out-perform The Horsemen in every way."

It seemed like common logic, he thought while glancing back and shrugging his shoulders. Hopefully, the crowd thought so too.

"Where are we to go from here?" Another question was thrown out from somewhere in the crowd.

David wanted to rub his head and tell the truth – that he hadn't a clue what the world would do from this moment forward. He was a scientist, not a fortuneteller. He was fumbling for words, and Alice cringed when she felt him slipping downhill. Unable to let him stand alone, she put her hand on his shoulder and gave it a squeeze. I'll take this one, she suggested with a smile. Appreciatively, he stood aside.

"The whole point of progressing mankind is so that you can all answer that question for yourselves. You can call us Creators. But when it comes to your lives and what you choose to do with them, you're the ones in charge. All we did in the lab was give you the tools to better yourselves. Now it's up to you to do with it what you will."

"The Quiet One thought She made us perfect the first time," a girl called out as the crowd parted uncomfortably around her. "And now you think you've got it right this time. What if you're wrong just like She was? What if we spend our entire lives knowing we'll never be good enough?"

From under the illuminating street lights, the girl moved forward slowly as if each step carried with it an invisible and unbearable weight. Wet, as if fresh from the shower, her hair was pulled back in a ponytail. Her gaze remained locked on The Creators, and they in turn wouldn't do her the injustice of looking away. She was seeking answers that even they couldn't give, but that was no reason not to try.

"We do our best," Alice told her comfortingly. "That's all any of us can do."

"If even Creators can't make us perfect, we're destined to try and fail." The crowd mumbled and whispered at her words. They weren't sparking disinterest, but rather fear that what she was saying might be true. "I don't want to keep failing," she insisted.

Before anyone knew what was happening, she lit a match that instantaneously set her whole body on fire. "She's covered in gas!" Someone yelled. The crowd shrieked in horror at the sight of the girl crying and screaming through the flames. "Someone help her!" The public shouted. "Someone help her!" But the inferno was already out of control.

The final scream penetrated the ear of every bystander as it suddenly came to an untimely end. The body fell to its knees before crippling over and resting its face on the ground. It was over while the fire still cooked. Sirens arrived while the cinders still glowed red.

EIGHTEEN

Seeing a young woman incinerated on the street would normally have a profound impact and warrant the attention of every press outlet for at least a week. But aside from those present, few others knew exactly what had happened.

The next morning's feature headline announced the first brutal death in what had overnight been deemed the War of Creation. It was dramatic, shocking, and kept all attention glued to the media for constant updates. Reporters silently patted themselves on the back for their undeterred commitment to the pursuit of public knowledge and true sensational journalism.

In order for citizens to feel safe and protect their families, they flocked to the human development clinics to receive the serum as soon as the doors were open. If a war was starting, no one could afford to be the only person left unenhanced. As promised, every person in the city had received the dosage within the week. And by the end of week two, the surrounding areas had almost been completed.

The effects of the serum were as indicated on the consent for development form. There was a brief period of increased temperature and nausea. This was to be expected while the body began its reconfiguration. Immediately following, the desire to sleep lasted for four to five days. When the individual finally awoke, the muscular system was redeveloped and the beginning protrusions of wings and a tail were visible. Though the tail took two and a half full weeks to fully develop, the wings required an additional two months of growth followed by another few weeks before they were strong enough to be used for flight with feathers grown to full length.

Practically overnight, the need for cars disappeared. The metro was all but empty. Only those with babies and small children still used public transportation. Everyone else chose to fly.

With so much happening and their newfound deity status that far superseded that of the average celebrity, David and Alice moved in together. It was easier this way. They had spent every waking moment together for so long and practically lived together already, leaving both their flats and relocating to a loft near the lab made sense. They nursed each other during the serum's fever phase and took turns looking after Milo while the other began the long sleep.

Though society as a whole followed the calcunist example and praised advancement and the benefits of daily life, The Horsemen used violence indiscriminately and at random. To demonstrate its progress in the war, the group opened fire on three nightclubs in a well-known calcunist district. It had the desired effect and gained massive attention. Two months later, the group bombed a fashion show that was unveiling new garments accommodating wings.

A week following, five department stores with similar outfits went up in smoke. 'This will not be tolerated' was the new slogan always found somewhere nearby.

In response to the growing threat, police did what they could to cope with the disasters and looked for anyone suspicious in the process. But singling out a culprit was all but impossible in a sea of panicked faces. More attacks followed which only frustrated law enforcement further.

After four months without a single solid lead, the first breakthrough came when two girls were caught trying to break into one of the newly constructed vaccination clinics. Curious enough to be the only two in the entire city without enhancements, suspicions were easily confirmed when a search of their carrying bags revealed enough explosives to destroy the entire building. The announcement of their capture was released immediately, and the city cheered feeling safe for the first time in over a year.

It didn't take long for The Horsemen to realize the flaw in its design and took steps to continue its efforts. By now, police were on the lookout for anyone still unenhanced. Such a person was easy enough to spot, and the public was instructed to call about anyone they knew fitting that description.

"We've all made the necessary enhancements," a spokesman for the group was quoted saying in a press release that displayed a photograph of a masked figure with wings and a tail. "You will not find us. We will do our duty, and then we will return to our original form."

The short news piece was all it took to rouse public interest and its unquenchable need for more information. In response to the hype, The Horsemen announced the creation of the Purist Theological Interest Group that held the same beliefs as themselves but was not affiliated with The Horsemen and its violent pursuits. Though there was heavy suspicion that key figures were Horsemen themselves and responsible for orchestrating attacks, not enough evidence could lead to a conviction. Without fear of arrest, members of the interest group put their faces in the spotlight for all to see and became regular guests on the news.

David found himself back in a familiar newsroom. Cameras were all around him, and the man seated on the other side of the anchorman was none other than Gordon Lowry, lead advocate for the Purist Theological Interest Group. Being in the same room with such a dangerous figure did not sit well, but Dresden Industries had urged there be at least one such conversation taking place to quell public demand. Though a Creator, David still earned his paycheck.

The mood was far from relaxed. Even the news crew behind the glass windows felt uneasy with such an arrangement. But as soon as the light signaled they had gone live, everyone put aside their apprehensions to get it over and done with.

"I can't officially comment for The Horsemen," Gordon said when the conversation shifted to the latest stream of attacks. "But as an advocate of purist ideology, it's quite easy for me to see how the forced progression of society has given the group reason to retaliate. And after the arrests, its members must feel compelled to look like the rest of us. The need for enhancements has certainly taken a toll on the group's structure probably causing some dissension between those who are willing to adapt to continue the war and those who see the act of receiving the enhancements as a form of betrayal to the true cause and subsequently give up the fight thereafter."

"That's a very good point," the anchorman commented, "and I believe one of the women arrested in the attempted clinic bombing wrote about this dissension quite a bit in her new book that's being published while she serves out the remainder of her prison term. But if The Horsemen isn't even decided how far is too far before the men and women betray their own cause, should we still allow it any credibility?"

"Absolutely. Like any denomination, there will be those who do not fully agree with the doctrine and will walk away. But for those who are devout followers of The Quiet One and Her message, they are the ones that remain and see things through to the end."

"The end is an ominous notion that strikes curiosity and panic into many of our viewer's minds when thinking about The Horsemen's ultimate agenda," the newsman said as a matter of fact. "But as your group adamantly follows The Quiet One and her beliefs, we have in society other groups that view the world differently. Just like The Quiet One, we have with us a Creator who has a very different outlook on this matter."

Gordon clenched his jaw at the mention of another creator. The sight of David was enough to cause him personal insult. At that moment, everyone in the room was grateful for the police stationed in and around the newsroom.

"Dr. Allens," the newsman continued. "I'm sure you and Dr. Clarke didn't intend to offend any group with the human development project or ruffle their feathers so to speak." He couldn't help but smile at his own humor. "So we're clear, what was your overall objective with the enhancements?"

"We wanted to give mankind a better way of living life," he said calmly and tried to look composed enough over the camera for Alice to feel at ease while she and Milo were down on the corner watching the news screen as well as the match on the larger television. We saw flaws with the fundamental design of our anatomy and fixed them."

"But some were offended by your choice to amend The Quiet One's work and took it as a personal insult against their faith," Gordon quickly blurted before the anchorman had time to intervene. "You, creators, are singlehandedly responsible for creating the discrimination against anyone who chooses not to be enhanced. You've created a world where one cannot function except by your standard."

"I feel compelled to interject to this point," the reporter said trying to keep the air from filling too high with tension. "It's my understanding that those not receiving enhancements found the stress of their lives greatly reduced for a time. From the reports we had after the first month of enhancements, the few who chose to remain without the serum didn't have to worry about over congestion on the metro, they were first in line at the vaccine clinics since no one else required them anymore, and they could drive the streets at rush hour with no more than five or six cars on the road at any given time in the entire city. But even those who resisted the change eventually came around when the benefits were all around them."

"It was forced," Gordon insisted. "Many felt compelled to take the serum after police were singling others like them out as criminals."

"After the city and all surrounding areas were enhanced," David said nonchalantly. "The Horsemen were the only ones left matching that description."

"So the real question here," the reporter interjected, "is whether or not The Horsemen's beliefs should be allowed the same standard of treatment as everyone else following its stream of radical behavior."

"Of course it should," David responded and watched as both Gordon and the reporter looked at him in complete surprise. "Just because we have enhancements doesn't mean we're doing away with the legal system and its protections."

"That's a valid point," the anchorman said while sifting through some papers. "I think a statement from the United Purist Congregation's founder, Stephan DaSilva, sums up this point quite well. 'All faiths exist to bring out the best in us. And if The Horsemen's beliefs bring meaning to their lives, then the practice has merit. But to the best of my knowledge, The Quiet One hasn't actually spoken to anyone or given the suggestion that She wants Her creation to be destroyed. Therefor their faith, as ours, should certainly be allowed, but it's how they choose to practice intolerance and act against other religions and purist denominations that can't be permitted.'"

"They'll do as they see necessary in the eyes of The Quiet One," Gordon said fervently. "And we can all be rest assured they will not stop until this enhancement has been put right. And then where will we be? Will the police again be apprehending the first who reverse their enhancements, or will it be those left altered that will be profiled?"

"Reversal?" David asked curiously. "They want to reverse the effects of the serum?"

Gordon let out a laugh as if he were trying to explain a complex notion to a child. "That's the only way back to the first moment of creation. We can't very well return to perfection while still walking around with wings and a tail."

David stared at the man and the condescending smile that accompanied. His eyes flashed to the camera. Was Alice watching this? Was she also dumbstruck? He knew Milo was with her in the pub – probably howling with the kind of laughter he never felt necessary to control. He looked back at Gordon and then to the reporter.

"Can I ask you to air your thoughts?" The reporter said trying to continue past the sudden moment of silence. "Do you think society will agree to reverse the enhancement process?"

David shook his head. "It can't be reversed," he said in a swoop that left the news eager for clarification. "When we enhanced, we removed the genetic sequencing that carried the imperfections. There isn't even a trace of it since the new sequencing overrode everything completely."

"So The Horsemen's agenda is not only unrealistic," the reporter commented, "it's impossible."

David gave a nod. "We've reached a point in human development where the only way forward was by removing the flaws in the original design altogether. We couldn't build on those pieces and maintain integrity throughout the entire genetic structure. So we had to make the choice either to progress or stay in the past. We chose to progress."

The Horsemen's advocate sat there without a word. His eyes filled with an unspoken contempt and frustration. Dreams crashed somewhere inside, and he folded his hands calmly.

Purism and his relationship with The Quiet One remained intact, but was Her message and call to action really as clear as his mind had made them out to be? Creation be damned – it would begin again. But this time, it would be done right. Why did She desire his intervention if the pursuit was doomed to fail from the beginning? For the first time that night, Gordon was speechless.

PART TWO

NINETEEN

Society was changing. With expanding potentials to be reached by the new human came a political demand for regulation. Grossly unpopular but with unlimited budgets, lobbyists stressed the need to know who was in the air at all times. They called for the creation of flight permits. Determined by price, the more money spent meant the more time one could spend in the air. Flying in business areas would be more expensive as would peak travel hours. Any politician who supported the endeavor knew a new level of wealth would be obtained overnight at the expense of being immediately removed from office due to popular demand.

Effective immediately, schools were required to comply with the new aviary program. Due to safety and security risks, flying was initially prohibited on school grounds. Though recess areas were surrounded by fences and walls which had once proved sufficient in keeping the children contained, such features were no longer enough. The aviary program turned schoolyards and playgrounds into domed cages. Once completed, students were able to stretch their wings in a more controlled environment.

Using a tail was practical for the simplest of tasks. No one used their hands anymore to press elevator buttons. Instead, the tail whipped around as if specifically designed for such a rudimentary task. Hands were reserved for better use.

Twisting tails became the new handshake that quickly spread from a young, new trend to the corporate world. Close friends continued to shake hands and greet each other with kisses; but for the new acquaintances, such a personal gesture was far too improper.

With tails entwined and hands joined, an older couple was out for an evening walk through the streets. Though flying remained the ideal way to travel, many found enjoyment stretching their legs and moving at a slower pace. They talked together and told stories. What had once been a necessity was now a treat.

New possibilities had brought about new ways to live, and society adapted at its own pace. Children with silly smiles hung upside down from their tails letting the blood turn their faces red. Cardio workouts at the local gym now included a slot for flappers which mixed dance moves and wing flapping with the latest songs. Hot flapping later developed when a gym's air conditioner broke and the trainer needed to explain away the hot and musty air to his uncomfortable class.

It was another casual Friday afternoon at Dresden Industries. Taking a break from work and enjoying gourmet sandwiches in The Rendezvous, David and Alice smiled politely to the public diners who filled their entire section of the restaurant and continued to glance at the Creators with amazement.

"Everyone eats," he told Alice casually. "You'd think they'd expect this from us from time to time."

"I think they're more awestruck just to be witnessing the event," she remarked through a smile. "It looks like one of them might try and take a picture. We'll be all over the internet within the hour."

From the corner of their eyes, they watched a man pull out his phone all the while glancing in their direction. It was difficult not to giggle, but Alice tried her best while David coughed into his napkin. They continued to wait feeling the tension rise until, at last, the pair looked at each other in confusion. The man hadn't moved.

"Did he already take the picture?" David asked.

"It looks like it. The whole table is looking at his phone."

David risked a glance only to feel his amusement instantly drain. Something wasn't quite right. Instead of the common enthusiasm derived from sharing such a moment, the group looked uneasy and agitated. A woman's eyes grew wide, and she covered her mouth in horror. Whatever they were looking at stirred David's curiosity.

It only took a second for David to realize that there was more than one phone in sight. Across the room, little by little, each table was pulling out a phone and staring at some mysterious image on the screen. Whatever it was, it was clear no one liked what they were seeing.

Alice squeezed David's hand to get his attention. Breaking him free of that unconscious need to stare, she glanced to the door and gestured for him to do the same. Already on his way over, Mr. Germond's assistant was halfway to their table by the time David got the hint.

"Doctors," Martin said with an uneasy smile. "I apologize for interrupting your lunch, but I'm afraid something urgent has come up."

"What's going on?" David asked before taking a final glance around the room.

"This really isn't the best place to talk. But Mr. Germond will explain everything in his office," Martin commented while taking a glance of his own.

Alice's phone began to ring. David's followed suit. Showing each other the numbers, they exchanged wary glances with instant recognition of the news reporters on the other ends.

"It's probably best talking with Mr. Germond first before getting in touch with the press," the assistant told them. More than happy to postpone an interview, they both declined the calls.

Without another word, they followed Martin out of the restaurant and to the elevators. As he walked, David felt the eyes of onlookers burrowing into his back. He continued forward and didn't venture another glance.

"Sorry for being so cryptic back there," Martin apologized once the three were secure behind closed doors. "But with the restaurant being open to the public today, saying anything in front of them would be a disaster."

"Please tell me we're not being scheduled for another interview," David said wearily.

"I wish it were that," Martin laughed anxiously. "We all know how to handle the press, but we'll be in new territory on this one."

"Martin," Alice said calmly. "What are we walking into? It's obviously important. Is there anything more you can tell us? I would really prefer not being caught off guard."

"I'll be honest with you," he said as the elevator doors opened and they walked briskly towards Mr. Germond's office. "You're going to get the same report that came to my desk fifteen minutes ago, but I have no idea how to even describe it. There's been an accident. Once you get all the details, maybe you can be the ones telling me what we're dealing. For The Quiet One's sake, Meghan is my godson's niece and she was right there! I can't even give her parents the peace of mind that this won't happen again!"

With a quick knock and without bothering to wait for a reply, Martin opened the door and escorted the two inside. Mr. Germond was talking quickly on the phone. As soon as they entered, he wrapped up his conversation at once. His assistant shut the door on the way out.

"Martin told us there's been an accident," Alice said as soon as the phone line went cold. "Is everyone alright?"

"Unfortunately, no," Mr. Germond told her in a shaky voice. "Three children and one adult died at the scene. Another child died on his way to the hospital. Two more have critical conditions, and three adults have a few scratches of their own."

"What happened?" David asked horrified.

"Haven't you checked the news?" The pair looked at each other and shook their heads. Without another word, Mr. Germond reached for a remote and switched on a television in the back of the room. The screen came alive to a special report airing live from Plensdam Elementary School.

"As you can see behind me," the news reporter said gesturing to the domed schoolyard over his shoulder, "the children had nowhere to go. Due to the newly developed aviary program that turns school play areas into cages, even the sky was no longer a way to escape.

"The recess monitor, Mrs. Sheill, was the first to notice what was happening," he continued." She pulled the creature away from the first victim. But before she knew what she was dealing with, it had turned on her and tore out her throat."

"We keep hearing about this creature," The news anchor commented. "But what exactly is it? Are we talking about a person with some irregular deformities or mental disabilities? Or is this some kind of wild animal gotten loose?"

"That's a good question," the reporter commented. "And I'm being told that an investigation is already underway to make that determination. At this point, no one wants to make premature assumptions what it was that killed those children. And after the attacker was shot and killed, the body was immediately taken away for examination. But from the video that a passerby took on her phone, we can clearly see that it more closely resembles a human than an animal."

The image shifted to a scene of the schoolyard where children were flying and screaming. Away from the flock, something followed behind and picked off the students one by one. Almost human but not quite, David and Alice couldn't quite figure out what exactly they were looking at. The image blurred every time the thing took down another body. Over the horrific cries of children, a piercing shriek came out of the perpetrator.

"Perhaps you can clarify the situation since I'm having a bit of trouble understanding what I'm seeing," the news anchor went on. "This video sent to us looks like it begins right after the first victim and continues for the duration of the attacks. How was she able to alert the authorities while capturing this footage?"

"The sad answer is that she wasn't," the reporter answered. "Had the woman alerted emergency services at the beginning, it's speculated that the death toll would've been cut in half. Because of this and the fact that she knowingly chose to record a crime instead of preventing others, she has been arrested and will be charged as an accessory to murder."

Mr. Germond switched off the television. For a moment, there was silence. After such traumatic news, the quiet was eerie. David wanted to speak but couldn't seem to find the words.

Thinking back to Martin's personal stake in the matter, Alice clasped her hands over her mouth in shock. "Is Meghan alright?"

"From what I've been told, she's understandably very shaken up. But she'll be fine."

"What exactly was that?" Alice asked knowing no one else was competing to be the first to speak. "Was that a science project gone wrong?"

"I was hoping you could tell me," Mr. Germond said nervously. "Due to the nature of this attack, the authorities are giving us access to the body. I'm told it has a number of bullet holes, but we should still be able to get some answers nonetheless. No one will say anything official, but I'm being told the attacker was human."

"How is that even possible?" David asked astonished. "It has the basic human shape, but you can clearly see it's something else entirely."

"You of all people know that playing with genes is a tricky business. One slip and the person is born without a lung. Throughout the entire human enhancement process, I've looked over the data and never saw a cause for alarm. But when something like this happens, I need to ask you two directly. Could the gene sequences have modified themselves to create this change all on their own? Are we in any way responsible?"

"No," David told him firmly. "Whatever this is, it isn't us."

"I'm glad to hear that. Can you be certain?"

"The gene sequences were created to get us to a specific point," Alice conferred. "If it was our mistake, we would be seeing abnormalities within the design. Like a person born with six fingers or an extra limb, we would be seeing an extra wing, two tails, or disabled appendages. But whatever that was," she said pointing to the television. "It has a completely different design. And if that isn't confirmation enough, look at its mannerisms. It was primal and hunted. We only modified the physical form. That person's mind was tampered with. I heard screeching, but I doubt whoever it was even still had the ability to talk."

"Thank you for giving me that reassurance," Mr. Germond told them. "Everyone is already beginning to point fingers. It'll be a relief to tell them this wasn't a mistake on our part. But we'll still need to examine the body and offer assistance to the investigation. Since this is unprecedented and you two are the experts in gene modification, I'd like to ask if you would be the ones to take a look."

"I don't think either of us has ever assisted a murder investigation," Alice told him uneasily. "We're better in a lab with a microscope."

"I know this is asking a lot, but my friends in law enforcement tell me that they're already at a dead end. They have the perpetrator, but making sense of what they're seeing his hopelessly out of their depth."

David sat quiet thinking things over. What he had just seen on the television frightened him;

but at the same time, he was fascinated. Why a person would do such a thing was beyond his understanding. Alice was right. The mind had been altered. He needed to see this for himself.

"Will they bring it to our lab?" He asked.

Mr. Germond shook his head. "It's at a morgue in Rhune, and every camera is aimed at the building. The police don't want to risk any pictures circulating which is why they'd like us to send our team there."

"I haven't been to Rhune in years," he said giving Alice a shrug of his shoulders. "When do we leave?"

TWENTY

It was a strange feeling leaving Ambris. David hadn't ventured out since he was a boy on holiday with his family. But then university started, and that was followed by work and more work. Since then, there had never been a dull moment nor a need for an escape. The city offered so many amenities - David was perfectly content right where he was.

Alice, on the other hand, had always felt a special connection with nature. Back before her father had gotten sick, she and her parents would hop in the car and drive to Lake Crescent for picnics at least twice a year. Stuck in the back seat with all the supplies, Alice's younger self had hated the commute. But looking back, she missed those days of simplicity and watching the sun set across the still water.

That cramped space in the backseat of her family's car no longer seemed so terrible, the woman thought as she and David continued to readjust themselves on the train linking Ambris to Rhune. While the rest of the world made adjustments to accommodate wings and a tail, the train industry clearly missed that memo.

The seats, cramped enough for passengers before the human enhancements came into effect, were now entirely unbearable. Along with the other passengers, Alice and David squirmed constantly. He suddenly winced and begged Alice not to move. She froze in place unsure of what had happened. Very carefully, David adjusted his back and pulled his wing out from between the seat and the center armrest that had somehow managed to come down on the appendage like a spike. He lifted it carefully and drew a quick breath when three of his feathers stayed attached to the ghastly torture device. Alice covered her mouth and tried not to look amused.

"It isn't funny," David told her. She nodded earnestly in acknowledgment and bit the inside of her cheek.

The train sped past the forests and through the farmlands. Gnarled, giant oaks grew in the valleys while towering sequoias separated the fertile lands from wine country. Even in the wilderness, each thing had its purpose. Some vegetation offered cover for animal life, others were a source of food. Trees marked unmistakable boundaries and gave structure to the fertile terrain.

Nearly six hours and five thousand miles later, the first signs of Rhune flew past the window. Snowcapped mountains and open fields were replaced by villages. Sparse at first, more and more took prominence until those in turn became a thing of the past with the arrival of suburbs. Passing through the sandstone arch that marked the train's entrance into the city, Alice and David pressed their noses to the window taking in the sights.

The city was old. Built on what was believed to be holy ground for both the purists and calcunists, each staked a claim to different sections of the city with various religious passages from each side etched onto plaques and displayed throughout. Sandstone buildings, erected centuries ago and updated over the years, lined the streets.

From what David could remember from his last visit when he was only seven years old, Central Square was supposedly the Rhune's foundation and the first spot to sprout buildings and thoroughfares on all sides. On one end, an enormous stature of The Quiet One stood tall for all to see. Dressed in ancient robes and standing forever alert to the surroundings, Her outstretched arms welcomed all. Pressing gently against the carefully chiseled fabric, a slight protrusion from Her stomach signified the birth of all things.

People came from all around to marvel at Her beauty, take photographs for holiday remembrances, or simply to pray. Many purists approached the statue in their best hat or scarf. They pressed their lips to the cold image and prayed for the blessings only She could bestow. More than a few covered their wings in a sign of shame.

On the opposite end of the square stood an ancient tree visible from the original city boundaries on all sides. Believed to be an extinct species, the seed had been discovered and modified to endure through the ages. With a base nearly fifty feet in diameter, its roots supposedly reached across the entire city. Evergreen leaves sprouting from monstrous branches provided constant shade. Ornately placed throughout, large white flowers blossomed giving the air a floral scent.

Comparatively, the giant image of The Quiet One was no match for the innovation of nature. But instead of anger at such a confrontation, She stood grateful, protected from the sun and allowing her worshippers to gather together in the shade. Purists let their children fly up to the tree branches and play their many games. Calcunists enjoyed the simplicity of The Quiet One Herself watching over their creation. While some naturally opposed such a sight, most of the city appreciated the arrangement.

As the pair disembarked the train, they watched as heads began turning in their direction.

At first a wandering glance, it wasn't until the second take that recognition made many eyes grow wide. Before long, a crowd had gathered and everyone with a camera was flashing away. Unable to find an opening, The Creators were forced to stand still, smile, and hope that things would settle down soon enough.

With tightly locked hands, they smiled calmly and tried to put on a pleasant face. They were responsible for the new world after all. Never spoken but universally understood, a Creator would never be too busy for the creation.

Alice's smile faltered for all but a moment when she felt a small but sharp pain on her wing. Not sure of what it was, she shook them gently. Another prick stirred her, and she looked over to see two of her feathers being coveted by the crowd. She moved a little closer to David unsure of what to do.

Before she had time to react, there were shouts of anger followed by the sound of a punch knocking the wind out of someone. The crowd had grown silent. Cameras had ceased to flash. From within the gathering, a man who looked to be in his late fifties walked forward with head lowered.

He stopped in front of the pair. His eyes looked into theirs before finding anchor with Alice. As if overcome with shame, he tried to hold her gaze only to find his head lowering and eyes moving toward the ground once more.

"I'm sorry, Mother," he said holding up the stolen feathers. "They had no right to take these."

Alice was taken by surprise. It was the first time she had ever been addressed as Mother. Her head spun trying to imagine why the people would think it necessary to bestow her with such a title. The man waited for her to speak - as did the crowd. All eyes were on her wondering what the Mother would do next. As diplomatic as possible, Alice gave the man a comforting smile.

"Thank you for returning them," she said watching the man's eyes lift and meet her gaze. "But I'll have to grow new ones since they can't be put back. Keep them. It's my way of saying thank you for helping me leave here without an entirely bare wing." She looked at the crowd with the same pleasant smile. "And I would appreciate it if no one else gets the idea to give me a plucking."

TWENTY-ONE

Aside from a group of mothers pushing strollers and a teenager being the laughing stock amongst his friends for having a broken wing, the metro was empty. Had it not been for their luggage, The Creators would've flown. But since neither one knew their way around by air, the metro got them to the hotel where they checked in and freshened up before heading out to dinner.

Videos from the train station had already been uploaded on the internet, and David sat at the restaurant playing one after another while Alice buried a red face in her hands. Video titles included "Mother Shows Mercy" and "WWMD - What Will Mother Do?" Alice reached for the phone and buried it deep in her pocket before David had the chance to click on a video titled "Mother is Real, and She's Beautiful."

"You know," Alice said once they returned to the hotel room for the night. "Even though we're here because people died, it's also nice to get away."

David smiled and watched as she tossed her clothes on a chair and searched through her luggage for the dark blue slip she slept in most nights. Her hair fell loose down the sides of her face and David watched as she tucked her bangs behind her ears only to have them come loose again a moment later.

Deep in concentration, Alice hadn't noticed the man come up behind her and wrap his arms around her waist. Feeling that satisfaction that warmed her to the core, she put the search on hold closing her eyes and smiling. Placing her hands on top of his, Alice leaned her head back against David's shoulder and enjoyed the feel of their embrace. His tail touched the back of her ankle moving up the calf and across her thigh. She took in a breath as it gently squeezed her flesh.

"Face it," she said through closed eyes. "You love me." She instantly felt laughter-filled kisses running along the side of her neck.

"I don't think I ever led you to believe otherwise," David said coming up for air before landing his lips on her skin once more.

"There was that one time when I wasn't sure what you thought of me," she said thinking back. David stopped mid kiss and turned his face to look at her.

"Which time was that?"

"It was just after I was enhanced. You were still the old you, and I was something new. I wasn't sure if you would like what you see."

David's arms squeezed her stomach a little tighter, and he watched her casually part her wings so his body could press tighter into hers. Her bottom made a slight adjustment when his body made contact.

"I guess that day was rough on both of us," David told her. Her body froze in surprise as she turned to face him. Small creases in her forehead marker her lack of understanding, and the curiosity patiently waited for David to explain.

"We had gotten that far together," he continued. "But then you were something new while I was still the same me." David faltered for a moment and looked down slightly embarrassed. "...I guess I just didn't want you starting your new life without me."

"There wasn't a chance of that, darling!" she assured him. "For me, it was a step we came to together. And that's how I wanted it to stay." She gave him a kiss and again felt his tail running along her thigh. "But what did you think? Did you prefer the old me or the new one?"

"That was just your insecurities, Alice, " he told her and felt the woman shrug her shoulders in agreement. "You were something special to me then, and I'm still just as crazy about you now. I already thought you were perfect before. And now there's even more of you to love." He kissed her bare shoulder before running his mouth up her neck and nibbling on her ear. The scent of honeysuckles filled his nostrils, and he happily breathed in her natural perfume.

The woman suddenly pulled away and turned to face him. With a playful look in her eyes, she put a hand on her hip and posed for man before her.

"More of me to love?" She repeated. "Do you love my calves?" She asked turning around so David had a clear view. Alice rose to her tiptoes and, with both hands on her hips, she spread her wings gracefully and shot the man an alluring smile over her shoulder.

"Yes," was all that came to mind until David remembered he knew more than one word. "Your calves are gorgeous."

"How about my wings?" she asked facing David. She crossed her legs and did the same with her arms while raising them high above her head. Her wings fanned out to the sides before draping around her body.

"Your wings are beautiful."

She bit her lip playfully and thought for a moment. Dropping a hand back to her hip, her tail found its way to the other. She began swinging it clockwise while pressing her lips together playfully. "Do you like my tail?"

David gave a nod. "It's the best tail I've ever seen."

Alice turned again and let her raised arms hinge at the elbows and rest on her shoulder blades. She looked innocently at the ceiling and let her wings drape forward. "And what about my ass?" She asked. "Do you like my ass?"

She felt a tug on her tail and shuffled backwards landing in David's embrace. With a smile on her face and laughter in her heart, she returned kiss with kiss with tails wrapped together for the entire night.

TWENTY-TWO

Anxious to get an early start, Detective Walter Matthers was at the hotel and waiting in the lobby promptly at eight in the morning. He was of course on official business, but having the opportunity to meet the Creators face to face was a highlight that would go down on his list of personal accomplishments.

As soon as he saw the pair descending in the glass elevator, the detective checked his tie and ran his sweaty palms down the sides of his jacket making sure it was wrinkle-free.

"You must be Doctors Allens and Clarke," he said inadvertently lowering his head. He extended his tail which the two gladly clasped it with their own. "I'm Detective Matthers. Mr. Germond told me you two will be able to give us some answers. ...Not that we needed Mr. Germond to vouch for you," he quickly added. "Your names alone are enough to give us every confidence in your abilities."

"It's nice to meet you, Detective Matthers," Alice said with a smile.

"Please," he insisted. "Call me Walter. I only make the criminals and my children call me detective."

"Your children?" David asked curiously.

The detective shrugged his shoulders. "Only when I'm cross with them. But enough about that. How was your trip? It wasn't too long I hope."

"The train got us here in no time at all," Alice told him. "But I know we'll both be celebrating the day the trains update their seating."

Walter nodded in acknowledgment. "I've heard stories about that from a few different people now. Word has it that the government is threatening to take over the entire rail unless change happens soon. With any luck, we won't have to wait much longer. Shall we get going?"

They nodded in agreement.

"The police still give me a car," he told the pair as they followed him outside. "But I'll be honest. It doesn't get much use now that flying is an option. And this way, I can tell my wife I'm getting some exercise. You know how women are wanting to make sure their men are in top shape," he said giving David a look of camaraderie. David stole a glance at Alice who was looking him up and down with a hidden smile.

They sped through the air all the while taking in the sights. With Walter in the lead, David and Alice followed closely behind. From high above, the giant splay of green and white on the tree seemed to stretch far and wide. Alice had never before seen the statue of The Quiet One and was desperate for a glimpse. But as they were there for a purpose, sightseeing would have to wait. They continued on until at last descending in front of the city's morgue.

"You might want to brace yourselves," Walter told them after they had checked in and found their way into a room with walled, refrigerated compartments. "It isn't exactly a pleasant face."

David's eyes flew wide the moment Walter pulled out the body. Alice frowned in confusion and looked at David for some kind of understanding. "I told you it was ghoulish," the detective said indifferently. "But what exactly it is, we're hoping you can tell us."

Even with the clear addition of human enhancements, the creature was far from ordinary. Instantly distinguishable as a she, her breasts and genitals were the only recognizable features amid a myriad of question marks. The woman's nails were closer to talons. Her skin was ghostly pale revealing every vein underneath. It was thick like leather and had accumulated unevenly across her body in patches.

From the mess along her metal bed, it was clear that the platinum feathers were coming free of their own accord. Staring at the wings, it took David less than a minute to spot an irregularity.

"What is it?" Alice asked noticing the frown across his forehead.

David took a step back and looked at the body in its entirety. "This woman has grayish-brown hair. Her feathers are the wrong color."

"Maybe she changed her hair color," the detective added unsure what such a detail could mean.

Alice shook her head. "If the hair genes were altered, the feathers would still reflect the change. The only way to separate the colors would be an external application like hair dye." She lifted the sheet exposing a dark mound of pubic hair. "But since the hair color is uniform across the entire body, we can cross hair dye off the list of possible explanations."

Walter scratched his head. "I'm afraid you've already lost me. How is this woman's hair color in any way relevant?"

"Different colors running through the same genes are evidence that there was genetic modification," David told him. "When we first heard the news, we weren't sure if the creature had been modified or if it was created this way."

"The fact that she was clearly out of her mind matched both theories," Alice added without taking her eyes off of the body.

"But now that we know what we're looking for," David continued. "We can figure out what happened to her."

"So this was just an ordinary woman until she decided to be her own creator," the detective said trying to wrap his head around things.

"That's one possibility," Alice remarked. "But considering we're standing over a corpse, it may not be that simple. She wasn't able to say a single word during the attacks which means her mind was already useless. I can't imagine anyone would voluntarily make the decision to lose her mind."

"This certainly adds more questions."

"With any luck," David commented. "We'll be able to give you some answers after we get her under the microscope."

From the cold, metal table, the woman's lifeless eyes stared blankly through clouded crimson rings. With fingerprints oddly absent, there was no immediate way of identifying her. Even her teeth had changed. What had once been an indistinguishable smile was now further cause for alarm. Her incisors grew jagged and at angles. The canines were abnormally large and digging into her lips. Even the molars were pointed and unruly. The transformation made Alice's stomach turn.

All morning was spent taking notes. From the unusual skin texture to the sixth toe beginning to form on both feet. Nothing was left out. The longer the body was examined, the more curious David became. It wasn't just a genetic modification - it was a complete disaster. He would have to wait until they started pulling samples to confirm, but the evidence already looked daunting.

When mid-afternoon rolled around, Walter forced them to take a break. Both were so engrossed in what they were doing that neither one noticed the passing hours.

"Come with me," the detective told them. "The body isn't going anywhere, and I'm guessing it'll look the exact same when we return. But for now, you both really should eat something. They say people are at their best when they're not working on empty stomachs. I know a very good spot with excellent kebabs. You can't come to Rhune without trying one."

Though the mystery of the woman brought about hundreds of questions all of which needed to be answered, it was true that they did need to eat. Alice had been the first to rise that morning and had ordered some eggs and toast for the room before getting ready. She had only taken a couple bites when she checked her watch and saw that they were running late.

David was even less fortunate. He had taken a sip of Alice's coffee and a few bites of her toast before rushing out the door. Between the two, lunch was definitely a good idea; and after hearing the occasional grumble from both empty stomachs, the detective figured now was as good of a time as any to take a break. The two peeled off their rubber gloves and cleaned up before stretching their wings and following Walter across the sky.

"When was the last time you were in the city?" Walter asked them as they soared over the many city districts.

"My last visit was when I was seven," David told him. "But it looks exactly the same as it did then. Maybe there's a few new restaurants, but the architecture looks about the same."

"We do appreciate the old," Walter confirmed. "It's part of our heritage and our identity. But we do keep up with the times. As you know from the body you're examining, even our crimes are very modern. What about you, Doctor Clarke? How long has it been since your last visit?"

"This is my first time here," she said with a polite smile.

The detective nodded in acknowledgement. There were so many occasions when she was younger that she had hoped to visit Rhune like so many of her friends had done. But her mother had always wiped away the very notion of such a holiday with a wave of her hand. Pointless, she had called it.

Calcunism teaches us to look forward, was the only explanation she offered. Why admire achievements that are already a thing of the past? Alice had never known how to answer. There was no answer ever good enough.

But she was here now. Perhaps it would only be a short visit, but that was good enough. Seeing the great tree drawing ever closer gave her the satisfaction of achieving a lifelong pursuit. Her eyes lit up when at last, she saw The Quiet One welcoming her with outstretched arms. But Central Square looked different from the pictures. The group descended, and Alice held her breath in shock at its entirety.

The Quiet One stood opposite the great tree, but she was no longer alone. Alice was there, and David as well. Cast in enormous statues, they stood opposite each other with outstretched wings. Landing in front of a restaurant terrace overlooking all three monuments, Walter watched with an amused smile as The Creators stared at their own image.

"This way," Walter told them leading the way into the restaurant.

On the restaurant's balcony under the shade of the great tree, the three sat at a table near the rail. Walter hadn't been exaggerating. The kebabs really were one of a kind. But as much as they enjoyed their meal, David and Alice couldn't help stealing glances at their giant selves.

"I have to ask," David voiced finally overcome by his curiosity. "When did those statues go up?"

"Why did they go up in the first place?" Alice shot in unable to keep silent any longer.

Walter looked at the two amusedly. "Why do you think the city would construct such statues in the first place, Doctor Clarke? To answer your questions, they are fairly new. After the last resident in the city got the enhancements, they decided statues were in order to mark the occasion."

"That's certainly nice of Rhune," Alice said trying to think of the kindest way to respond. "But did they have to put us right next to The Quiet One

Herself? That seems a little presumptuous. Don't you think?"

"We are called Creators," her partner commented casually.

"That's not helping."

"Doctor Allens is right," the detective said finding obvious humor in the situation. "You are known as The Creators for a reason. And in Rhune, we call you Mother and Father. At the heart of things, we're a very religious group. We've never before had those walking among us who are responsible for all that we are. Maybe the statues were a publicity stunt - I really don't know. But I can tell you that we all look at those statues and feel gratitude for the gifts that have been given to us."

"They're not very lifelike," David said with a frown. "I don't think they even gave us tails."

Alice closed her eyes and let out a deep breath. "They're probably hiding under the robes."

TWENTY-THREE

A full day in the morgue had made their heads spin. They were used to examining genes that in turn led to a physical form. It was unconventional to be working in the reverse order.

What they were discovering was already unnerving. It had come as even more of a shock when Walter's phone rang and his face turned pale. There had been another attack. This time in Ambris. A dimly lit concert hall had led to the deaths of over a dozen people. With so much cheer and music bouncing off the walls, many had died before the room finally realized what was happening. Shot to death by security, another mysterious creature was laid on ice.

Calling Mr. Germond, David made arrangements for Alice to examine the second corpse. He insisted on staying behind - something which Alice was by no means happy about. All of their work had been done together. Suddenly separating without even asking her what she thought of the idea was out of the ordinary and not like David at all. Something about this whole situation was making Alice more uneasy by the minute.

"I really need you back in Ambris," David insisted as he brought Alice to the train station. "You're the only one who can make sense of my notes. And by the time you get back, hopefully I'll be able to tell you what to look for."

"We could pass along the same notes to anyone at Dresden," Alice said sensing the uneasiness in David's manner and knowing there was more to it than just convenience. "What's really on your mind, David? I know when something's bothering you so don't try and hide it."

"It just has to be you," he insisted with absolute sincerity. "Please ...please trust me this once. I really need you there." She knew David well enough to know when he didn't want to concede. This was one of those occasions. The woman could push as much as she wanted, but David would hold his ground. "Please trust me on this," he repeated.

Pursing her lips, Alice let out a sigh and nodded in compliance. "But you will have some explaining to do when you get home," she insisted. David smiled and, pulling her into his arms, kissed her forehead.

There was no sense to be made of the situation, but Alice still had many hours to think it over the entire trip back. Traveling alone did present her with the opportunity to spread out across two seats instead of one, but she would've gladly exchanged the extra wing room for the comfort of having David close by.

Why did he have to be so difficult? Of course she trusted him. She would've gladly sailed to the far side of the world if David had told her to do so. She was committed and knew wholeheartedly that he would always put her above anything and everything else. But an explanation still would've been nice. Alice tried closing her eyes to keep her thoughts from spinning.

It was already well into the afternoon by the time Alice reached Ambris. Arriving on the platform, she stepped off the train to find two men holding up a sign with her name waiting for her. Surprised by the welcoming party, she made her way across the platform to see what they wanted.

"Doctor Clarke?" One of them said with a reassuring smile.

She gave a nod. "That's me. What is this all about?"

"Mr. Germond sent us. We're your security detail to take you straight to the lab. We have a car waiting just outside. Can I take your bag?"

She handed over the bag all the while trying to wrap her head around this. Something was definitely wrong. First David was acting peculiar and insisted she get out of Rhune, and then a security detail to be her personal escort? Alarm bells were sounding in every corner of her head, but nothing seemed to indicate the need for such extreme measures.

Once in the car, she picked up her phone and immediately called David. There was no answer. Leaving a message and thinking for a moment, she tried Mr. Germond's office. "Hi Martin," she said hoping to brush through the formalities and get some answers. "Is Mr. Germond around?"

"He's in a meeting at the moment," Martin told her. "I saw that your train arrived a few minutes ago. Has the security service found you?"

"That's actually why I'm calling. I'm with them now, and they're taking me to the lab. What's going on?"

Mr. Germond's assistant paused for a moment before responding. "It was David's idea," he said as if giving a confession. "He said it's urgent you get to the lab and to make sure you arrive here safely."

"Did he offer an explanation?"

"He was in a hurry to get back to the body," Martin told her. "David made sure you were taken care of and then went right back to work. You know how he gets when he's focused. But he thought you getting here in one piece was important enough to tear him away from the work to make the arrangements."

Alice did know David's personality - especially when he was immersed in a project. The details consumed him and stayed on his mind until every variable was clear in his mind. But this was different. It was clear how curious he was by the body, and he surely would've kept at it until answers began to present themselves. But the look on his face at the train station wasn't the distant gaze that came from calculations - it was worry. She wanted to be wrong but knew well enough, he was afraid. Without any traffic, the car reached Dresden Industries in no time.

Alice stopped as she entered the lab. Calvin was there. Sitting on a stool staring at the lifeless corpse on the table, his arms were folded around his stomach as if the sight of such a creature was nauseating.

"Calvin, what are you doing here?" Alice asked as she set her bag on the desk.

"We can finally get started," he said excitedly. "David called me and said you'll be needing an extra pair of hands."

"He did, did he? Why do I feel like he's talking to everyone but me?"

"I don't know about that," Calvin commented lifting a chart from the edge of the table. "He sent this over less than an hour ago and said it's for you."

Anxious for answers, Alice grabbed it with a bit too much excitement and muttered a quick apology before skimming the information feverishly. It was a detailed dissection of the woman back in Rhune. David had worked fast and focused on specific body parts. Attached to the last page, there was a note written in David's hand.

Hi honey, I'm glad you made it back safe. Rhune wasn't safe for you, and I needed to get you out of here in a hurry. Thank you for trusting me. I know it's been a long trip, but I need you to work in a hurry. I've attached what looks like modified gene sequences. Check for the same ones on the second body and their maturity levels. I'm sorry I can't be there to give you a hand. Calvin is more than capable to be your gopher on this one. Concentrate on the stomach and lungs. I love you.

"The stomach and lungs," Alice repeated David's words aloud.

"I saw that too," Calvin said casually. "If we're doing a dissection, those are certainly odd places to start. Any idea what he's after?"

At once, she grabbed two surgical masks. Handing one to Calvin, she put the second on right away. More than a little confused, Calvin did the same. Alice knew David's thinking pattern. And giving Calvin a nod, she pulled a pair of surgical scrubs out of a drawer and threw them over her clothes.

"Whatever caused the change," she said while putting on a pair of rubber gloves. "David thinks it might've been airborne or ingested. That's why he wants us to check those organs first."

"He's brilliant, I'll give him that," Calvin admitted. "But how would he even know to look there?"

Alice shook her head. "I think he's the only one who can answer that."

Knowing exactly what to look for was like playing connect-the-dots. David had given them the information. All they needed to do was confirm that the same modification process used on the last attacker applied to this one as well. The answers were easy enough to find. While the lungs had changed at the same rate as the rest of the body, the stomach had begun the process far earlier.

The lungs are clean, Alice wrote in a message to David. "But you're right. It's in the stomach. She had barely set her phone down on the desk when it began to ring. David's name appeared on the screen. Relieved to be hearing his voice, she picked up at once.

"It's about time," she told him playfully. "I thought you were going to keep me waiting all day."

"I missed you too," he told her, and Alice felt relief at the sound of those words. "I've been at it nonstop on this end. Otherwise I would've called you sooner."

"I figured as much. But don't kill yourself, David. You may be a Creator, but you still need to rest." She could hear the wear in his voice and hoped he at least found something for dinner.

"I won't be at it for much longer," he told her solemnly.

Alice was about to ask about his progress when words suddenly failed her. The door to the lab had opened and instantly making herself at home was her mother. She said a quick hello all the while draping her coat on a chair and checking the state of her hair.

"You're Martha Clarke," Calvin said trying to keep his enthusiasm in check. "It's an honor to meet you."

"Of course it is," she said nonchalantly. "But I don't know who you are."

"You'll never guess who decided now was a good time for a visit," Alice said into the phone.

"That must mean Martha arrived," David commented taking her by surprise.

Her eyebrows lowered into a frown. "David, why is my mother here?" She asked already knowing the answer. She clenched her jaw when he confirmed her suspicions.

"I asked her to come."

Alice looked vexingly at the woman who was already taking the liberty of putting on one of her lab coats and glancing through computer files. She and David would be having a serious talk as soon as he got home.

"I know how you feel, and I wouldn't have done it if it wasn't important," he assured her sensing the woman's disapproval thousands of miles away.

"You'll have to start giving me some answers," she insisted. "Up until this point, I've been more than understanding. You told me to leave Rhune - I did. You ordered security - I didn't make a fuss. But now my mother is in our lab - our lab, David. You know how much she wanted this. Why would you invite her?"

"...Because I'm sick," David told her. She was taking in a breath and felt it catch in her throat.

Her mouth fell open as her eyes filled with panic. Alice shook her head and smiled while a hot tear escaped from her eye.

"No, you're not," she corrected at once. "I was with you this morning, and you were fine. If you have a headache, it's probably from working for so long without a break. Why would you even say such a thing? Are you trying to scare me?"

From the other side of the phone, David's voice was caught. It was a struggle saying it out loud, let alone to the one person he would do anything to never let down. But she had a right to know. Since they first met, he had never kept a single secret from her. David wasn't about to start now.

"It was in the coffee," he said forcing the words out. "Back at the hotel, you had the eggs, and I took your coffee. You have no idea how thankful I am that you went without caffeine that morning. I felt a little strange ever since. But I didn't realize what was happening until I noticed a few of my feathers going pale last night."

"Are you feeling alright?" Alice asked already trying to think of ways to get back to Rhune. "I can be there by tomorrow morning."

"Don't you dare," he said sternly. "That coffee was sent to our room which means we were targeted. I can't risk anything happening to you."

"How did you know it was the coffee?"

"We left the dishes in the room that morning," he said with a hint of laughter in his voice. "When I took it to the morgue, it still had a dose of whatever serum was added. That's the one piece of luck we get out of this. We have the serum. I sent the details to our lab computers."

Alice let out a desperate laugh. "At least we have that. "David," she said trying desperately to hold back the flood of tears. "You need to come home so we can figure this out."

"That's not an option," he said sadly. "I'm a safety risk. There's no telling when I'll start attacking people. It really is only a matter of time. You know that."

"But you're alone. I should be there with you."

"I'm alright," David told her trying to put some optimism in his voice. "Walter is going to lock me up, but he assures me that he'll also keep me safe. That's the best anyone can do right now. Look after Milo for me. I'm really sorry it has to be like this."

"You're apologizing even though you're the one being locked up?" She asked incredulously. "What sense does that make? I'm going to fix this."

"I know you will," he said comfortingly. "But while you're at it, try to take it easy on your mother. She's there to help in her own egotistical way."

Alice clenched her jaw and took a deep breath. "No promises."

TWENTY-FOUR

Mr. Germond had been in meetings all morning. Moving suspicion away from Dresden Industries was easier said than done. Reviewing the facts with officials confirmed the company was entirely innocent, but the press had launched its own campaign of suspicion.

If the human development project hadn't been news enough, breaking stories of the attacks fueled a wave of bottom feeders. Everyone had an opinion. Some shouted government conspiracy while others were certain it was a global pandemic. Taking a quick break before his next appointment arrived, Mr. Germond turned on the television to see a discussion panel already well into speculation.

"...So you're telling me that the attacks weren't caused by a pandemic," the news anchor said with curiously.

"If you want the truth," the visitor that the screen identified as Corwin Blake: author of Our Genealogy Gone Wrong. "You have to look at the facts. What we know is that two related incidents have taken place in very different locations. With so much distance between them, we can rule out any kind of disease otherwise we would be seeing clusters of similar occurrences around both attack sites."

"But there are none," the news anchor told him and watched as the man nodded in agreement. "Does this mean we're leading more towards the possibility of conspiracy that these creatures were some kind of test subjects that accidentally escaped? If that's the case, it would be no wonder why the genetic laboratories haven't acknowledged their involvement in both situations."

The man laughed mildly and scratched the back of his hand. "I love conspiracy theories as much as the next person, Simon. But I'm afraid that one is a bit far-fetched. Two laboratories in different cities losing dangerous specimens within the same week would be more than coincidental and entirely improbable if you really think about it."

"Then we can rule out the mad scientist theory."

Taking a deep breath, the man shook his head and closed his eyes solemnly. As if trying to find the words to deliver the sad truth, his returned his attention to the news anchor with obvious understanding that he was to be the bearer of bad news.

"Genetic modification facilities and companies like Dresden Industries were not the perpetrators of the attacks, but they are responsible for the creatures themselves." With eyes glued to the screen, Mr. Germond motioned for complete silence as Martin entered with a stack of reports. "Anyone who's seen footage from the attacks knows that those creatures were, at one time, people. We know they were entirely unrelated. This means that the only thing they had in common was that both attackers had at some point received the human enhancement serum."

"Are you suggesting that their serums were tainted with something else?"

"Absolutely not," the man said at once. "With so much security after The Horsemen incidents, I don't think it would even be possible for its members to get within a mile of where the serum was stored - and then again when a separate shipment was distributed to Rhune."

"But as you suggest," the news anchor pressed. "The serum is the source. If it wasn't tampered with, how does this explain what we've seen?"

"If you've read my book," he said holding up a copy for the camera. "You'll realize that genetic modifications are anything but clear and simple. Changing a gene sequence can of course alter the physical form, but one slip is all it takes and a miracle turns into a disaster. We've all been eager participants taking the serum and progressing to this new point, but what we are now seeing is the next stage of our development because the serum is not done changing us."

The news studio was silent. Mr. Germond and Martin forgot to breathe. The words were sinking in with the full weight of what the man was suggesting. The news anchor looked at Corwin Blake with shock and horror. He tried to compose himself, but it was of little use.

"That's a very strong accusation to make," he said still trying to steady himself. "But if we all took the same serum, why are we only seeing these two cases instead of millions?"

"That's a very good question, Simon. And the answer has to do with time. Maybe the bodies of these two individuals went through the enhancement process quicker than everyone else. If that's the case, they would naturally be the first to start showing signs of what is to come. But one thing is for certain. As more time passes, we will start seeing more cases."

"If this is the case," the news anchor thought out loud. "Then anyone could potentially become one of those creatures at any time."

"Unfortunately, you're right. This is what happens when creators alter The Quiet One's perfection. It's a losing battle for humanity, and those responsible really should be held accountable."

"We would expect to hear such things from a purism extremist," the news anchor commented. "But I've been told that that part of your life is over. We are aware that your name was among those arrested a few months back for attending a Horsemen rally. Can you comment on that so we can give your words the consideration they deserve and know there is no longer any bias on your part?"

"I would be glad to," he said scratching the back of one hand to the point where it was becoming red. "Writing a book means I have to investigate the subject from all sides. Going to a Horsemen rally was my way of showing impartiality in my work. But as you can see, I'm not wearing a hat. And I'm no more a Horsemen supporter than I am a purist."

Mr. Germond muted the program. "Please tell me you have good news," he said looking at his assistant and trying to force a smile.

"Actually, I do." Martin paused when the sound of his phone began ringing ominously. "Your appointment with the next city official cancelled since she felt Dresden Industries was innocent of any wrongdoing."

With a hand on his forehead, the director shook his head listening to the sound of that incessant ringing. "That would be Diane changing her mind again. No doubt she just saw the interview and is already contacting lawyers."

Martin frowned in confusion. "But I thought it's already confirmed Dresden Industries couldn't have had any part in the attacks."

"That's entirely true. And for anyone willing to look at the data, they'll come to the same conclusion. But this isn't about facts," he said pointing to Corwin Blake's muted image on the screen. "That man is acting on the grounds of wild speculation. And he's inciting a global panic in the process! Mark my words, the public will be demanding blood, and this book-writer just became the face leading the charge. I would have our Creators give a live broadcast clearing all of us from these accusations, but one of them is currently in the process of becoming one of those things while the other is in no state to speak to anyone. Things are going from bad to worse."

The sound of papers echoed as they crashed to the floor, and Mr. Germond looked up to see his assistant was dumbstruck.

"I'm sorry, Martin," Mr. Germond said immediately. "I meant to tell you right away but then the meetings and phone calls started."

The phone on Martin's desk continued to ring, but it was irrelevant in the man's mind. "How did this happen? I just spoke with David a few hours ago. He didn't say anything at all."

"You know David," Mr. Germond said rising and helping his stunned assistant into a chair. "Once he realized what was happening, his only concern was getting Alice as far away as possible. He's a genius, but he's also a romantic. He only started looking into his own condition after he was certain Alice was out of harm's way."

"She never would've left if she'd known," Martin thought aloud while thinking back to her calm tone over the phone.

"No," he agreed. "That's why David kept it a secret. And to think, the cause was in a morning cup of coffee delivered right to their hotel room!"

The assistant's lowered head suddenly popped up to attention. The whole situation was unbelievable, but to deliver a dangerous substance in such a well-populated place was boldly foolish. "That hotel is filled with security cameras."

"Detective Matthers already had the same idea. Apparently, that morning's footage is missing from the records."

"How can I help?" Martin asked at once. "Do you want me to make arrangements to bring David back?"

"That's not necessary," Mr. Germond told him. "The detective has David locked up for now which is for the best to keep him out of the news. He'll be kept safe as will the public. Alice is leading a team to do what she can from the lab. What David needs from us is to handle everything else.

Public opinion is turning The Creators into the most hated people on the planet. We have to find a way to turn it around."

TWENTY-FIVE

The clipboard fell to the floor as Alice suddenly realized her hands were trembling. She couldn't breathe. The room was closing in around her, and there was no escape. Terror filled the woman's eyes, and her legs buckled before she found herself on the floor.

"Alice!" Calvin said at once. "Are you alright?"

She couldn't speak. The thought of what was happening was too much to handle. How could she keep working knowing David might never be the same again? When his body passes a certain point, would he still recognize her? Even worse, would she still recognize him? These questions brought a new onset of tears that could not be controlled.

"I can't..." she told Calvin. "I just can't"

There was a tap on his shoulder, and Calvin looked up to see Martha gesturing for him to get back to work. I'll handle this, Martha told him with a single look. She's my daughter, and I know what she needs. Nodding in acknowledgement, Calvin returned to his seat in front of the computer all the while watching as Martha finally came down to her daughter's level.

"This is the worst part of it," Martha said while cautiously patting her daughter's head like an unpredictable pet. "Today is the hardest day, but it does get easier."

"How will it get easier?" Alice retorted incredulously amid the sobs.

"You'll cry off and on for weeks, but then you'll figure out how to live without him. It won't be easy, of course. But practice your calcunism, and that will help the time pass quicker."

"You're acting like David's already dead. He's not," Alice reminded her. "He's still David.

Even after he's changed, David will still be somewhere in there trying to come back to the surface."

"You need to pull yourself together because thinking like that isn't going to solve anything. You're a Creator. You still need to act like one even when disaster strikes. David knew what was going to happen and did everything he could to get you back here safely so you could come back to this lab and find a way to stop a very real problem. It's too late for him. Since he really did care about you, I wish things had turned out differently. But this is life, and Creator or not, you can't change what's already been done. David's last act as himself was helping you, so don't fall apart now and have it go to waste. You need to get up, keep breathing, and live up to his expectations."

The words tore through her like thorns. Alice's heart was bleeding in a way she never thought possible. David wasn't dead; he was still alive. How dare her mother come in here and act like he was already crossed off! She wanted to yell and scream at the top of her lungs. It would at least be temporary relief to smash every glass instrument in the lab as hard as she could against the walls.

Getting up with as much dignity as she could muster, Alice pulled one of David's old handkerchiefs out of a drawer and wiped away her tears. She couldn't help but smile and even laugh as the cruel reality of the situation set in. Her mother stood before her, silent but watching at the unpredictable creature before her. Alice felt anger rising to the surface at the sight of Martha's very presence.

"You wanted this all along," Alice said in disgust. "You've been waiting for something like this to happen from the beginning. You're not a Creator, and David chose to work with me, a nobody, over you, the famous Martha Clarke! But if he's out of the picture, that leaves a spot open. What did you think? That you can just come in here and take his place? It's not going to happen."

"You need to pull yourself together," Martha repeated with a rueful eye.

"Then answer me this," Alice began with a glare that comes from the onset of victory. "If David is dead, why are you here? He was the one who invited you in the first place! You're playing both sides accepting his offer and making a move to replace him in the process! Our names are on the lab door. I have no intention of adding yours!"

"I'm not here to work," Martha shot back while looking away uncomfortably at the sound of her own confession. "I'm here for you." The woman's eyes glanced time and again towards her daughter's disbelieving face before finally finding the courage to look her in the eyes. "David didn't ask me here to work on a cure. Ask yourself, does that even sound like him? The man has an unhealthy obsession with you and asked me to come because he knew it was a lost cause. Even though you and I share many disagreements, David thought my daughter would be needing her mother during the worst of it."

"Then why are you wearing a wearing my lab coat?"

Martha looked at the garment and shrugged her shoulders. "If your mind is busy with other things, you're not falling apart. And since I'm here to help, I might as well make use of my time."

The unpleasant truth wasn't as piercing as Alice had first encountered. Instead, it felt like a shackle taking her deeper and deeper below the surface. She was drowning. The pain caused her senses to go numb. Even now, her awareness of the world was becoming nothing more than a blur.

TWENTY-SIX

From his seat at the desk, Calvin couldn't believe what he was hearing. She was wrong. Martha Clarke had always been one of his role models, but she was still wrong. He knew it in his heart.

Ever since university, he and David had always looked out for each other. Even after the bomb blast when the thought of ever again setting foot on a lab floor felt impossible, it had been David who had gotten him a job at Dresden with some of the best security in the entire city. It had given Calvin the confidence to carry on.

Now that their circumstances were reversed and it was David who was in an impossible situation, Calvin wasn't about to let his friend be ruled out as a lost cause so easily. Pieces of the data looked familiar. If that wasn't encouragement enough, there was the certainty that he and Alice would stop at nothing to get him back.

"David's not gone," Calvin suddenly remarked and instantly received a stern look from Mrs. Clarke. "We can't do anything about the change, but he's certainly not a lost cause." The light had already faded from Alice's eyes, but she lifted her head as a final attempt at finding hope.

"David sent us the data on whatever was in his coffee," the man continued. "I'm not the expert in the room. But from what I can tell, the brain isn't permanently altered or damaged. Before this cushy job, I did my fair share of regrowing limbs to replace damaged ones. This looks like it has similar gene sequences to block transmissions to the brain. We used ours to block pain receptors, but this one looks like it was designed to block entire regions. If that's the case, then David isn't gone - he's just losing access to the more developed areas of his mind."

"That all sounds well and good," Martha said irritably. "But it's a lot of wishful thinking."

"I would bet money on it," he said fervently.

"Then it's no wonder your name isn't on the door either."

"If you think we can get him back," Alice said trying to keep calm, "I'll believe you."

"Alice," her mother said pointing to the lifeless creature on the table. "Look at this. Whatever it is, it certainly isn't The Quiet One's perfect creation in need of a little help becoming something better. It's a disaster! There is no rhyme or reason to a single aspect of its design, and David is going to be the same way. You can make a serum to block the mutations so no one else will suffer, but it's useless once they've already reached this point."

"It is a disaster," Alice said thinking all the while taking in every detail of the creature before her.

"That's a start. Now do something useful. Keep David in your heart and focus on what's important right now."

Alice shook her head. "You don't understand," she said as the wheels in her head began turning after a temporary suspension. "It's a disaster because there is no solid design. Blocking access to the brain looks like the only thing that was precise. Everything else doesn't have an ounce of sense. What am I missing? David and I would find it easily, but I can't make heads or tails of what I'm seeing."

Calvin walked over while Martha crossed her arms and contributed the occasional glance. From the uneven layers of skin to slight bone protrusions under the skin, Alice took in every detail. Mrs. Clarke shook her head in disapproval. Although Calvin wanted to be helpful, he had no idea where to begin.

Try to think, Alice told herself. She looked the creature up and down all the while silently asking David for the answer. She imagined she was back in Rhune. David was still with her. The body before them was the first attacker. Examining the body, David was as fascinated as ever.

What is it? She asked the emptiness curiously. There was no response. David continued to stare. It's a disaster, she told herself. Don't you think? A light came in her eyes with sudden understanding.

"The wings," she said at last. Both her mother and Calvin looked at her curiously. "David saw it, but he didn't know what he was seeing. The answer is in the wings!"

"I'm not following," Martha said closing her eyes and feeling her patience beginning to waiver.

"The feathers are a different color than the hair. We know it's an indication that the genes were altered, but giving a person two colors on the same gene line is a complete waste of time. It couldn't be deliberate. Like everything else, it just happened.

"So someone changed the wing color by accident?" Calvin asked making a face and scratching his shoulder.

"The original feather sequence David and I used must've come from a platinum feather. That's why it's a consistency on both bodies and on David. We added a blocker so a person's natural hair color will be dominant and carried over during feather growth, but it's not present here. The same goes for every one of these features. We added so many new genetics to the mix that if you take away the blockers, they would overrun the body." She pointed to the body. "This is exactly what would happen if genetic alterations continued without a clear ending point. The only purpose in this design is to let the newly incorporated genes take over and completely overwhelm the body."

"That's not really much of a design," Calvin remarked. "And if that's all we're seeing, then what's the point of any of it?"

"You need to be sure about this," Martha told her daughter seriously. "What you're suggesting is that someone is intentionally unlocking gene sequences to run wild. From what I heard on my way here, you're not very popular at the moment. The only way anyone will listen is if you can prove what you're saying and offer the solution at the same time."

"Then that's what I'll do," Alice told her. "David wanted me in the lab, so this is where I'll be.

I can run computer simulations to prove this is what's happening. And in the meantime, I'll get started restructuring the gene blockers so whatever was in that coffee will be rendered useless. And then I can concentrate on David."

"I'm your extra pair of hands," Calvin told her. "I'm not an expert on creativity; but give me a list of instructions, and I'll follow them to the letter."

"Be realistic for a moment," Martha urged her. "You're used to working with a perfect model and keeping it neat and clean the whole way through. This genetic coding will look like someone put it through a blender. Blocking the gene growth isn't something that can be done overnight. And by the time you get it right, there's no telling how far gone David will be at that point." She lifted her nose to the corpse. "This is what happens after only a few days. There's no telling what you'll be dealing with after months."

"We'll face that hurdle when we get there," Calvin said adamantly. Alice nodded in agreement.

"What am I getting myself into?" Martha said before taking a deep breath and grabbing the clipboard on the desk. Without a word, she began pouring over the information while Alice and Calvin watched her curiously. "Mother, what are you doing?" Alice asked.

The woman looked up with the same irritable look Alice had seen so many times while being distracted from her work. "You may be a Creator, sweetheart, but I doubt you can fix this mess before the year is up. And don't give me that look, Calvin. You said it yourself that creativity isn't part of your repertoire. If you want your man back, you're going to need someone with enough finesse to salvage what little is left from a gene pool filled with sludge. And I promised David I would be here for you. So stop distracting me while I'm playing the part of the caring and supportive mother."

At a loss for words, Alice knew she would never understand her mother. Their minds were too different. What she needed explained, Martha considered common sense. Years of feeling inferior and repressed kept Alice at a distance from that woman. But in one act of what was anything but selfish, forgiveness was possible.

"And who knows," Martha added without looking up from the clipboard. "Maybe I'll get a book deal for what it was like saving the world and a Creator."

TWENTY-SEVEN

The month was already half gone, but public opinion remained firmly against the culprits of their demise. The calcunists were really to blame, it was decided. Had it not been for their persistent need for progress, none of this would've happened. If the Creators hadn't risen from those truly despised ranks, the world would still be at peace. Yes, it was their fault. There was no doubt about it.

Acts of arson sprung up in multiple clinics throughout the city. Few police cared to respond. Many in law enforcement had reached their own conclusions, and they no longer protected an institution bent on global catastrophe.

Terribly overwhelmed and going entire days without sleep, Mr. Germond had taken over press interviews in hopes of correcting a growing and dangerous misunderstanding. Though extraordinary behind a desk, he was by no means as remarkable in front of the cameras. One after another, news reporters spun his words to that of a monster.

Though it gave the press and the public great pleasure condemning the director and bestowing upon him responsibility for a world gone wrong, they were only getting started. It was the Creators they were really after, and it vexed them when neither one was present to accept their blame.

In response to so much hatred, some calcunists chose to convert to purism. After all, maybe the purists had predicted such a disaster in the first place. Instead of being harassed in the streets, others donned hats and scarves over their heads in a desperate attempt to better fit in. Though the practice worked for many, some of the more well-known calcunists trying this tactic were publicly identified as hypocrites and beaten to the ground by a pack of youths.

As Corwin Blake had predicted in his book, more creatures began appearing in the most unpredictable of places. One appeared in the middle of a park. Another attacked during the morning commute. One was found in her office. Unable to perform the simplest of functions, the transformed woman scratched and beat at the door all the while screeching at the top of her lungs. Contained but dangerous, law enforcement shot her on site.

When anyone could change without a moment's notice, the world became suspicious. No one spoke of it in public, but every eye glanced at the many posters and billboards displaying a special emergency response unit of government along with its phone number. Created by none other than Gordon Lowry, it was a place where anonymous tips could alert the police to people suspected of demonstrating creature-like behaviors. The press exalted the endeavor as keeping society safe. Though the majority were calcunist and high-profile public figures, nobody dared question what became of them.

Amid so much anger, panic, and suspicion rose a new way to prove one's true loyalty. Whether the practice began as an act of devotion in a purist temple or as a dare in a bar, no one knew for certain. But for those brave enough to repent for their mistake, they walked the streets standing proud without wings or a tail. Removed in the most medieval of ways, they left behind scars that The Quiet One Herself would be able to recognize. And when the rumor spread that such mutilation would prevent any chance of evolving into a mindless mutation, many picked up on the practice.

Away from the world and even taking their meals in the lab, Alice and the others continued to work. Milo's bed was set in the corner of the lab, but he preferred making himself comfortable on the chairs and in the middle of the walkways. They slept in the offices and worked around the clock. Venturing outside was not an option.

News of David was always the same. He was contained but safe. Detective Matthers had seen to that. Though Alice had only met him on the one occasion, she was forever in his debt for keeping

David's presence a secret and taking care of the man she loved. Her David was barely recognizable. In a different body and out of his mind, remaining alive and in the current condition had destroyed his body more than any other had experienced. But even with such information, Alice still hoped.

After the ninth week in the lab and too tired to see straight, Alice pulled off her gloves and took the escalator to the main lobby. Mr. Germond was there already waiting for her. Taking one look and expressing obvious concern over the paleness of her skin, he gave the woman an encouraging smile as he walked with her to meet the press and the cameras.

TWENTY-EIGHT

"Where's Martin?" Alice asked seeing that every person in the building was present except Mr. Germond's assistant.

"He had to take a last-minute train to Rhune," the director told her. "Something important came up."

"Is he going to see David?" She asked with sudden excitement.

"I'm afraid not," he said shaking his head. "But don't worry. I spoke with the detective earlier this week and was assured David is still with us ...in some form. Martin had to tend to a family matter but should be back soon."

Alice was nervous. It had been a while since she last had contact with anyone from outside. The cameras added to her anxiety. Her body seemed to be radiating honeysuckles from every pore. Though only a couple dozen news reporters had been invited, she could feel the hostility of the world being directed onto her as she took her place behind the podium.

Her hands were trembling. She wanted to put them in her pockets but knew that probably wouldn't be appropriate. She had prepared a few words, but her mind was going blank. With so many eyes on her, Alice told herself to keep breathing.

"There's been a lot of confusion about what we're actually seeing in the world," she began.

"There's no confusion," one reporter shot back instantly and watched as many nodded in approval. "You and your partner thought you could challenge The Quiet One and lost! Every dead body is on your hands!"

Cheers erupted from within the ranks while security took a step closer as a precaution. What do you have to say, they shouted. Alice tried to speak again only to have her voice be silenced by more cries of anger and resentment. After all she and the others had done to fix a problem that was never their fault, she was about to be crucified. The reality of the situation made her snap. Diplomacy be damned, she thought indifferently and gave the angry crowd a menacing grin.

"Here," she said taking a small vial from her lab coat and throwing it as hard as she could at the reporter's forehead. The man let out a wail as it missed its mark and knocked out a front tooth. "If you want someone to blame, find the person who created that!"

"You'll regret this if it's the last thing I do," the reporter countered while wiping the blood from his chin.

"It may well be the last thing you do if any of that liquid was ingested," she shot back menacingly. "That's the stuff that changes a person into an animal. It shouldn't take long before you can't even remember your own name. And after a few days, you'll be a problem. But don't worry. I'm sure the emergency services will take care of everything."

The man's face filled with terror. The room began to adjust as other reporters distanced themselves from him and the unbroken vial lying on the ground. Few bothered to take pictures. Most were eyeing the many security guards around the room uncomfortably.

"If you're going to be mad at someone," Alice continued. "Start with the person who created that. It didn't come from Dresden Industries and certainly wasn't a mistake of mine or Doctor Allens. But if you do want to see what we've been up to," she said pulling a second vial from her other pocket. "We've been working nonstop to keep you all safe. So if you'd rather hate me and don't want the serum to keep from changing into one of those things, the exit is right over there. I would say good luck, but you don't deserve it."

There was silence as the man stared at the vial in Alice's hand. He wanted it more than anything, but asking was too difficult. Few cameras dared flash, and Alice knew the photo of her holding their only salvation to a genetic disaster would be the top story within hours. Unable to control himself any longer, the reporter began to beg for the anecdote. Alice looked at him with disgust.

"You accuse me of destroying the world and then ask for our help right after," she said disdainfully. "Make up your mind because you can't have it both ways. Either we're destroying you or saving your life. Pick one."

"He had no way of knowing, Doctor Clarke," another reporter worked up the courage to speak and instantly regretted it when Alice directed her glare on him.

"He had no way of knowing even though Mr. Germond told all of you what was happening months ago? If you're still looking for answers after he already gave you all the facts, then you're really no good as a reporter. You might try for a profession that requires less thinking."

"I think what Doctor Clarke means to say," Mr. Germond took over with a smile as he stood by Alice at the podium, "Is that no one at Dresden

Industries is responsible for what's been happening to the public. And we have ample amounts of data to support this. But what our Creators have given us is a way to be certain no one else in society will fall victim to whoever is perpetrating this heinous crime."

"That's exactly what I meant to say," She said giving the director a fake smile while clenching her jaw.

"Now if you would all like to be caught up to speed, I can walk you through every detail until everyone here is satisfied. And then instead of asking for our heads, you might find your efforts better spent pressuring law enforcement to find the real culprit."

"If you'll all excuse me," Alice said with the same fake smile. "I have some more serum to produce." Without a single look, she walked over to the reporter with the bleeding face and picked up the undamaged vial off the ground. Returning it to her pocket, she let out a huff and turned. "Come with me," she said to the panicking reporter. "I'll give you a dose of the anecdote just in case. And while we're at it, we'll also grow you a new tooth."

"Mother," a female reporter called out as Alice was walking away. The Creator stopped and turned. "I'm sorry I didn't believe you."

Unsure of what to do but still too perturbed to respond with anything unhostile, Alice looked her in the eyes reproachfully. But there was too much sincerity to stay angry. And in that moment, The Creator wanted to cry. Alice gave her a nod of acknowledgment before walking away.

TWENTY-NINE

It was already after dark when Martin finally made it to the base of The Great Tree in Rhune. He had arrived in the city two days ago and had scarcely slept a wink. He wasn't there to relax. On this particular trip, he was here for a purpose.

He had met with Detective Matthers at the train station. From there, they had retraced Walter's steps going over everything he knew about The Creators' arrival in the city and the circumstances that had kept David in a locked cage ever since. The coffee cup had been the only bit of evidence gathered, but that alone was an impossible trail to follow.

Nighttime patrons frequented the surrounding restaurants. Some dined on the balcony appreciating the splendor of Central Square in a different lighting. Martin tipped his hat in their direction and continued waiting patiently for his guest to arrive. He checked his watch and looked around. Right on time, a dark figure walked towards him with all the swagger that youth allows.

"I'm glad to see you, Gregory," Martin said to his godson with a smile that couldn't remove the sorrow from his eyes. "But what did you do to yourself?"

"Oh, this?" Gregory asked glancing over his shoulder at the absence of wings and a tail. "It takes me back to my purist roots. I'm surprised you haven't done it yet."

Martin smiled at him incredulously. "Why on earth would I ever do such a thing to myself? The Quiet One loves her creation. She would never demand us to mutilate ourselves to be in Her good graces. Surely you learned that at the temple right around the time you learned to walk."

"Times change," the young man countered. "And The Quiet One demands more of us than ever before."

"That may be true. But striving to earn Her love through your pain is nothing more than righteous masochism. You're better than that."

Gregory shrugged his shoulders. He wasn't the sort to encourage such a trivial conversation. He knew what he believed, and it wasn't for even family to tell him otherwise. He looked at the newest statues of the Creators that graced Central Square and let the corners of his mouth sag of their own accord.

"I really thought they would've taken these down by now. After all those creatures started popping up, you would think the Creators would've been executed by now."

"Didn't you hear the news?" Martin asked. "Those creatures were someone else's creation. The Creators had nothing to do with it. In fact, it's taken them all this time to make an anecdote to a serum that's been wreaking havoc on the population."

Gregory's eyes went wide. He had been expecting Martin to defend the Creators to end of time but not to put them back on a pedestal as humanity's salvation. The idea made him sick to even think about.

There was a chill in the air. Even in the early months of summer, a cool wind from the north came down and mixed with the heat. The hot and cold reminded Gregory of two sides that would never be satisfied until the other was gone without a trace.

"Why did you do it?" Martin asked with an intense interest. The young man looked at him with confusion. "Why did you think taking lives would solve anything?"

"I think you have me confused with someone else."

"I want to hear it from your mouth," Martin persisted. "There's no point in lying since everything leads back to you. So be honest with me for once in your life. Was it worth having so many deaths on your hands?"

Gregory adjusted his hat and shrugged his shoulders. Even now, he couldn't say whether or not his efforts would pay off. But at least the seed of doubt had been planted which was what he told himself he was after.

"It's quite the assumption to think I have blood on my hands," he commented casually. "And finding proof that I had anything to do with a single death isn't likely. Police have been investigating the attacks for months. If they're empty-handed, I seriously doubt you'll do much better."

"You were the one who recommended the hotel to me when I was making reservations for the Creators. You used to work as a clinic assist which is why your serum only creates chaos. Maybe if you paid a bit more attention to the real scientists, you would've learned a thing or two."

"What makes you think it was intended to act any differently? The Creators changed the world. But as soon as creation turned to madness, those scientists became the most hated people on the planet. I'm not the only one in this city without wings. The Horsemen couldn't rally the people, but one slip up from the Creators and wings started coming off."

"Like I told you," Martin said with growing disgust. "They've fixed your mess. The serum is useless. You might as well use it as mouthwash since it now has no other purpose."

"I'll alter the formula. If I did it once, I can do it again."

"You're not that clever, and you know it, Gregory. Once was all it took to make sure someone with your skillset won't be able to use the same trick. But what I can't understand is Helen. She was your niece's babysitter. Meghan could've been killed! You realize that, don't you?"

"Like I told you," Gregory said raising his chin a little higher in the air. "The Quiet One demands many things from us. We all make sacrifices in Her name. It was unfortunate, but even from afar She kept Meghan safe."

"Then tell me," Martin commented while taking off his hat. Instantly, police flew out of the restaurants and appeared from every corner. The young man's first impulse was to fly away before he remembered his wings had been clipped. "Where's your sacrifice in all of this? Other people have died and yet you seem untouched. Why do others have to be sacrificed for you to prove your devotion?"

"You can answer if you'd like," Detective Matthers said while putting the young man in handcuffs. "But I don't need to hear a single word to make a case against you."

"I've done nothing wrong," Gregory demanded with a smile. "And you're arresting me because I'm a purist without wings. Is this the way you treat anyone who chooses to look different than you?"

"He's cocky. I'll give him that," Walter said. Martin took one last look at his godson and shook his head. "While you've been out enjoying this family reunion with your godfather, we've executed a search warrant on your apartment. And I have to say, anyone with half a brain would know not to leave so much evidence in plain sight.

"We've collected more than a dozen vials of a very questionable substance. If it turns out to be the serum used to target members of the population, that alone would be enough to keep you in a cell for life. But on top of that, you kept blueprints of the clinics that were bombed and a service uniform from the hotel where someone contaminated a cup of coffee served to a Creator. Were you planning to one day show the world your accomplishments?"

"You have no idea what an inspiration those actions are," he said lividly. "More will follow in my footsteps because of how far I've gone."

"Yes," Walter said with a roll of his eyes. "Many have reached out to you, and we do have a complete list. Honestly, keeping a special book of all your contacts was one more foolish thing to add to the list. We also have access to your phone and computer histories. Between those things, we should be quite busy for the next week or two."

Unable to have the final word, Gregory stared angrily at the detective hoping to make a lasting impression. After all that had been accomplished, he refused to be beaten. The plan had been perfect. The police had no reason to ever suspect a nobody. He shot his godfather a nasty look and cursed the man under his breath. If it hadn't been for that traitor, the world would be better off. Led away in handcuffs, he walked under the shadow of David's mighty wing.

THIRTY

Following Mother's memorable appearance that had indeed turned her and her team into the saviors of the world, the winds of public opinion started blowing in the opposite direction. Murderous eyes that once demanded her demise now lined up with heads lowered in front of alteration clinics in hopes of receiving the widely sought-after anecdote. They waited patiently all the while hoping no one would recognize them as outspoken purist advocates who had, on multiple occasions, publicly sworn to never again step foot in another clinic for the rest of their lives.

While Alice's absence from the public eye was viewed as anger towards how quickly society had spun out of control, it was actually due to indifference. David's condition remained a secret - it was better that way. People hoped for their forgiveness all the while listening to Mrs. Clarke's point of view as she graciously took center stage in the spotlight.

As Martha continued to tell the public, all of course would be forgiven but only when the time was right. Lives had been lost, people had disappeared, and neighbors were hunting neighbors. She couldn't officially speak for the Creators; but Mrs. Clarke assured the world that as the mother to the pair and a fellow savior of the world, she understood the Creators' thoughts that were still too painful to voice.

As hoped, Martha's fame grew. Finding momentum in the wake of things, she and several board members from progressive scientific companies launched The Religious Acceptance and Mediation for the Advancement of Humanity governmental department or RAMAH for short. Endorsed by Dresden Industries and the Creators themselves, RAMAH gained instant popularity.

Standing firm on the belief that science would continue to change the world for the better, its function was to hear from the religious views that were opposed to the changes and find a way to peacefully move forward.

As a first order of business, RAMAH called for the dismantlement of emergency response units. It was argued that with the distribution of the anecdote, such a service was no longer needed. Few opposed such a measure – especially after one of its founders, Gordon Lowry, had been charged with conspiracy after several calls were discovered taking place between him and Gregory Güttnem who had been universally recognized as the most despised person on the planet.

When it was finally safe for all religions to be visible in public, many in the cities put their hats and scarves away for good. The camouflage had kept them alive; but without the threat of persecution, they could once again walk the streets as proud calcunists.

For many, the work of the saviors and that of the Creators was inspirational. Some converted to calcunism as a result while others simply found the courage to visit an enhancement clinic to have their wings and tail restored. Being without them had been fashionable in some circles for a time, but it also proved to be terribly inconvenient. And when the true culprit had been within their ranks, no one wanted any association with such an individual. In addition, shaking hands with complete strangers was not something to be done in polite society.

As the world returned to normal and police took their duties seriously once again, Alice and Milo returned home in the evenings and tried their best to keep the apartment in a state that David would recognize. On the nightstand, his reading materials mixed with hers. The blanket they had used to cuddle together on the couch was folded neatly and waiting off to the side. The man's satchel still hung by the door. A pair of his glasses were still on the kitchen countertop. Alice occasionally cleaned under them and dusted them off but would never move such a sacred object.

Each morning, she and Milo made the morning commute to work. Milo had his own carrying bag and had mixed feelings that came with the sensation of flying. Though the goggles protected his eyes from the wind, he still appreciated the moment they landed and he could tear them away with a paw.

It was never made official, but Calvin split his work hours in his own lab and with Alice. Little by little, they made progress towards the reversal of David's condition. Once the anecdote was created, a vial was immediately sent to Rhune. The Creator was sedated and administered the serum preventing any further changes from taking place. Then it was a matter of returning him back to his former self - a simple enough task that presented a world of difficulties.

Sometimes, Alice and Calvin worked days in silence. Other times, they took their lunches together glad to have company despite the slow progress in the lab. Neither one would give up on David, and that simple fact gave them encouragement to continue.

Though Martha had her hands full with public appearances and political life, she kept her word to David and continued to be there for her daughter. Mrs. Clarke helped in the lab which seemed to be the only way she and her daughter could really connect. And instead of feeling threatened when her mother found a solution to what seemed to be an impossible genetic anomaly, Alice was grateful.

For some reason, Alice found it difficult to voice her gratitude. Instead, her mother arrived one afternoon to find that her daughter had hung an extra lab coat on the wall. Dr. Martha Clarke was stitched in blue letters above the front breast pocket. Martha looked on it with satisfaction and continued about the lab without saying a word.

Five months passed as winter quickly approached. Christmas was just around the corner, and the city of Ambris was filled with street decorations and outdoor holiday markets. During a time to be shared with loved ones, the team was finally ready to make a long-anticipated phone call to Walter. Prepare for her arrival, Alice told him. She was on her way.

Returning to Rhune where the memories came flooding back, the woman tried her best to keep ever-trickling tears from running down her face. In her pocket, she clutched the vial that had taken her so long to prepare. The uncomfortable train ride didn't even bother her. Alice's only thoughts were with Davis.

Not wasting any time, she met Walter at the train station and immediately crossed the city to a small police station on the outskirts of Rhune. Guarded by a select few the detective trusted with his life, a creature slept in a cell under heavy sedation. Alice covered her mouth as her eyes were filled with horror.

She had known David was changed, but seeing it in real life was so much more different than looking through a microscope. He was a deformity. Pale feathers had come loose of their accord, and his fingers and toes bled from uncontrollable talon growth. His teeth had made several slices through his lips, and the man's limbs curved in awkward directions unsure of which way to grow. Alice wiped her eyes and administered the serum without saying a word.

The only thing to do was wait. She didn't want to look at him but never dared look away. Maybe Alice could've done more if she had stayed in the city. She put that thought aside immediately knowing it wouldn't help. The woman was grateful he had kept her safe. But at the same time, she needed her David back. The hours dragged on, and the sedation continued.

When his mind returned, David screamed in pain. "Sedate me, sedate me!" He cried. David tried to smile when he saw Alice's face standing over him, but the pain throughout his body caused the man to lose consciousness before he could. Granting his request, Alice gave him another dose after dose of sedation. He slept without a sound for five days straight.

THIRTY-ONE

It took two and a half months for the deformities to correct themselves. David's skin peeled away multiple times before a healthy layer finally came to the surface. Every feather was entirely new since the old ones had dropped off while he slept. After so long being unaware of the passing time, it felt good returning to his old self. Renting an apartment not far from the station, it felt good having a comfortable place to recover and put some distance between himself and his holding cell.

The man tried not to voice it, but Alice could tell he was embarrassed she had seen him in such a horrific light. He had been at his very worst, and no man takes pleasure in the love of his life being uncertain whether to cry out of frustration or horror. "It's alright," Alice had told him one morning after breakfast. "I'm just glad to have you back." The scent of honeysuckles was a constant source of calm.

David's face had returned to normal, but the thought that kissing Alice would make her aware of some unseen scar or abnormality kept him at a distance. After all that he'd put her through, the man didn't want to disappoint her. But Alice didn't have the patience for such nonsense. Her lips found his time and again with all the intensity of an addict going through months of withdrawals. David was cautious at first, but soon they were laughing together, crying together, and appreciating the familiarity of being back in each other's arms.

When David was finally well enough and looked no different than when he first arrived in Rhune, the couple made plans to return to Ambris. On the night before their departure, he and Alice had Walter and his entire family over for dinner. Unsure of how else to express gratitude for all the detective had done for them, they were glad to find the meal was more than enough.

Walter was more than happy to be social after so many months of watching David deteriorate and being unable to do more. His family, on the other hand, was in awe at meeting the Creators. Several pictures were taken, and Walter's youngest son was even brave enough to sing The Glory of Mother and Father that his teacher had taught the class just as every other school in the city was now doing. Alice and David kept their tails entwined behind their seats never willing to let the other go.

It was well into the afternoon by the time their train reached Ambris, and the Creators walked hand in hand through the station. Heads immediately turned, and flashing lights came from anyone with a camera. They had been away from the press for months, and no one had heard a word from either of them since Mother's Rage as her last interview came to be called across the internet. Before the crowds had a chance to gather and start a stream of endless questions that would keep the pair answering for hours, David and Alice were already in the air and soaring past the billboard announcing Mrs. Clarke's book release, Creation's Guidance: Answering the Global Cry for Help.

Returning to their apartment, it felt good being home again. Milo was overcome with excitement. His whole body wiggled with joy all the while trying to cover David in kisses. Unsure if she would feel left out, he switched to Alice's lap and repeated the process all over again.

"Calvin dropped me off this morning," Milo told them. "I wanted to be here when you arrived."

"Alice told me you've been staying with him while she was away," David said rubbing his friend's ears. "It wasn't too awkward, was it?"

"Not at all," Milo assured them between panting and smiling. "We have a great thing going! He takes me to the pub to see the matches, and in exchange I let women pet me so he can get to know them."

David couldn't help but laugh, and Alice was too surprised to keep her eyes the same size. "How long has this been going on?" She asked wondering whether or not Calvin was a bad influence on the closest thing she had to a child.

"These things are so hard to remember," he said coyly. "I'll have to think about it and get back to you. But enough about me. How was Rhune? I saw your statues on television. Did you take pictures posing in front of them?"

"I think we must've forgotten to do that," David said giving Alice a grin.

"Oh well," Milo said hopping off the woman's lap and smelling whatever had been in her pocket. "You know, they didn't even bother to give you tails."

"That's what I said!" David agreed enthusiastically finding pleasure in no longer being the only one to notice the obvious. Alice rolled her eyes in amusement.

"I don't know about you two," she said casually. "But I'm starving and don't really feel like cooking. What do you think? Should we take a trip down to the pub?" Milo agreed instantly while David gave a nod.

Without a match being aired, the pub was all but empty. There were several empty tables to choose from, and they were given complimentary meals for having been gone for so long. Perhaps it was because the bartender had been one of the unlucky few forced to regrow his wings and tail after someone convinced him that it was the only way to keep from changing. Whatever the reason, they were more than happy to accept.

After so many months apart, they were finally a family again. Alice looked at her two boys in appreciation all the while keeping her tail wrapped around David's. This is how it's supposed to be, she thought with pride. She smiled to herself when David's hand rubbed her thigh under the table.

Filled from a good meal and enjoying a bottle of wine, they sat together on the couch while Milo had already sleepily disappeared into the bedroom. Alice drew the blanket over them and nestled up against David's body. They were both exhausted from a long day of travel, but neither one was ready to call it a night. They sat and talked all the while savoring the feeling of being back home.

"I never asked," Alice began curiously. "But why do you still wear glasses?" The question took David by surprise. After being together for so long and seeing each other change from limited to achieving flight, not once had the question ever come up. "Reconfiguring your vision could've been done ages ago. And when you grew a new eye, I kept it as an exact replica of the one you lost rather than take the doctor's advice and give you an upgrade. I don't know why I did that," she confessed. "But it seemed important at the time."

"I'm glad you did," David said moving his hand gently over her hip. "It's easy enough to do away with any physical flaws, but I like knowing there's some part of myself that's left to chance. Since you brought it up, why do you still wear glasses?"

"It's the same for me," Alice said with a gentle smile. "I could've changed it just like I could've gotten rid of my honeysuckle smell long ago, but I chose to keep both. I don't want to be a doll," she admitted. "And I always hoped that if I was lucky enough to have someone special in my life, he'd be willing to accept me with all of my quirks and imperfections."

David pressed his nose against her neck and inhaled deeply. "I more than accept you, Alice. I can't imagine changing a single thing about you. You were perfect the first day I saw you in the elevator, and you're just as beautiful now."

Alice felt a warmth radiating from her core and let out a giggle as David's lips met her neck. "Does that mean you like my neck?" She asked playfully.

"Very much."

"How about my ears?" she said feeling him nibble on one.

"Absolutely."

"And my tail? Do you like my tail?"

David turned her around so he could look in her eyes. Completely enamored, there were no words that could ever express all that they felt. It was a miracle that they had found each other.

Despite a world of controlled perfection, they had found all they needed from what was already there.

"Of course I like your tail," David told her meaning much more than he said. Smiling from ear to ear, Alice understood and let out a giggle. Covering them in the shadow of her wings, she let the moment take them both to new heights.

About the Author

Jason Medici is a California native. He earned his masters from the University of Nottingham before returning to the United States. To see his full range of books and to learn more, visit:

www.jasonmedici.com.